The Star We Share
ja huss

The Star We Share
Ja Huss

ABOUT THE BOOK

The bad boy cursed me, the control freak collared me, the golden boy kissed me—and I'm here for all of it!

I woke up in jail with three men fighting over who gets to claim me—and none of them are even human. Number One is a leather-clad demigod with a belt that does more than hold up his jeans. Number Two is a rogue secret agent with a habit of giving orders like he expects to be obeyed. Number Three is a flirty charmer who's convinced I'm his soulmate.

Apparently, I'm part of some ancient prophecy—the missing piece in a divine war. The gods want me back, the Titans want me gone, and these three lunatics are stuck with me in a death-trap labyrinth. To escape, we'll need to unlock our shared powers. Together.

THE STAR WE SHARE is a high-heat, fast-burn why-choose romance where Greek gods meet modern spice. Expect sharp banter, mythic danger, and a maze full of magic, mayhem, and multiple happily-ever-afters.

Inside the pages you'll find:
Why Choose
Enemies to Lovers
Fated Mates
Hidden Identity
Forced Proximity
Touch Her and Die
Ancient Gods and Goddesses
Quest/Labyrinth Adventure
Power Dynamics
Fantasy Spice
Found Family
Cursed Artifacts

1 - STAR

I dream of the earworm wriggling its way through my head. I can hear the music and even some of the lyrics, but none of it makes sense. It's like I'm underwater or listening through a wall.

The words are there—like *right* there. But I can't make them out.

So I invent lyrics to the melody in my head.

Make your bed and tip the sky?

The way you live is the way you die?

Except, that's not it. That's definitely not it.

Tie your shoe and skip the rope?

Beans are good and corn is dope?

The more I try to figure it out, the more ridiculous my attempts to decipher the muffled words become.

Dig your way into the sun?

Oh, forget it.

Anyway, it's morning, I guess. My back hurts and why is it so loud in my apartment? I bring a hand up to my head, pressing it against my temple, because I have a raging headache.

This is when I hear a man's voice and I sit straight up in bed, holding the covers close to my chest just to be extra special sure that no one's getting a peek at me.

Which is when I realize I'm not in bed. I'm not even at home. In fact, I don't know where I am. A small room made of cinderblocks with a toilet in the corner.

"Holy shit." These words come out as a croaked whisper as I spastically brush hair out of my eyes. "I'm in jail."

"You're in jail, *baby!*" These words, and the accompanying laugh, overpower all the other noises. I look in the direction of the voice and find a man leaning into the bars of the cell across the corridor. "Welcome back, Sleeping Beauty! Did you have a good rest?"

"Who the hell are you?"

"Star, I'm going to have to advise you not to talk to this man." This other voice comes from a second man, who slides into my view and pushes the other guy out of the way. "We don't know who he's working for and—"

"What's this 'we' shit," the first guy says. "You two are not a 'we'. We're a 'we', right Star?"

I brush more hair out of my eyes, as if this might clarify things for me, but, of course, it doesn't. So I just mumble, "What the fuck is happening?"

Now both of them squint at me.

"You don't remember?" the second one says.

"Are you sure?" the first one asks.

"Because," the second one says, "we had a deal and I'm fully expecting you to honor it."

"Bro," the first one says, pushing him away. "Shut the fuck up. There was no deal." He turns his attention to me. "Star, I know I came on a little strong last night, but we had a good thing going, remember? We were gonna go back to my place and—"

I'm shaking my head at him while he continues to talk because while I might've gotten drunk enough to get arrested and blackout, I am *not* a one-night-stand kind of girl. Not at all.

However... as he continues to explain how he and I are a team, I actually process his allure for the first time and start to doubt my certainty. Because holy fuck, this man is hot. Like something out of a myth.

Maybe a little lanky for my tastes, but lanky in a muscular way too. Like a swimmer, everything about him is *long*. And his shirt is ripped straight down the middle, affording me a perfect view of his equally ripped abs. The whole moment is like a spell. A little magic that lures my eye down to a teasing bit of blond happy-trail just above the waistband of his jeans. My eyes pause there for a moment as my mind catches up.

He laughs. It's a nice laugh and it comes with an equally charming smile. "See. You remember now, right?" Then he cups his hand over his mouth and whisper yells, "We wrote a little song about it." He does a weird jerky point to his happy-trail and then breaks into song. The exact melody I was humming in my head just before I woke up. The exact tune that's been haunting me since I was twelve years old.

Except, like mine, his words are all wrong.

"Take a step—one, two, three. Down the trail, you'll find my beast!" Then he beams at me. Like he's Mozart or something.

"For fuck's sake," the other guy says, pushing the first one out of the way. This guy couldn't be more different from Happy Trail. He's tall too, but he's not sporting a ripped body—at the very least, he's not showing it off with a ripped shirt. Because he's wearing a black suit. I'm talking tie, coat, button-down, and shiny black shoes. The whole shebang.

His hair is short and dark and so is the perfectly groomed stubble on his square, clenched jaw. But the darkest thing about him are the sunglasses over his eyes. They're the kind of dark sunglasses only blind people wear, but even though I've only been looking at him for a few moments, he's definitely not blind. It's very clear that he can see.

"Star," he says, his voice low and commanding. "I'm so sorry you're here. But don't worry. It'll all be over as soon as..." His eyes shift left and right and he lowers his voice. "Just as soon as you and I have a little chat. Don't listen to this guy's lies."

Who the hell wears sunglasses that dark inside?

A spark goes off in my brain and suddenly, I have a sputter of creativity and words fall into my head, fitting with the melody of the earworm tune. "Da, da, dahhh, da, da, da, *lies*. Yes! *Lies*! *Yeeeeees*!"

But that's just the first clue. Because as soon as that comes out of my mouth, part of the other line also pops into place. "Something... something... something... *eyes*! Lies and eyes! Yes! YES!"

"What the hell is she talking about? And why is she looking at us like that?"

I blink and find myself still staring at Sunglasses.

Happy Trail shuffles his way in front of him. "Because it's part of the song, you idiot." Then he looks at me. "You remember then? We were working on the song. So we could get the hell out of here?" He side-eyes Sunglasses, then growls, "Just the *two* of us."

I point to myself. "I was working on the song with *you?*" Then I scoff. "I don't even know you. I would never tell a stranger about my song."

He kinda grits his teeth here, then spits some low, whispered words through them. "That's because we're not strangers, Star. I came here to get you and you agreed to come with me because we were making progress."

"I can hear you, ya know." Sunglasses straightens his sunglasses and then lets out a breath and looks directly back at me. His words all very calm and rational. "Star, you're not going anywhere with him. You're coming with me. We had an agreement."

"How do I have an agreement with both of you? And can someone please tell me why I'm in jail!"

Happy Trail points to my left. "Ask him."

Sunglasses agrees. "Yeah. Ask him. He's the reason we're *all* in jail."

My eyes slide over to the left where Happy Trail is pointing, but I have to get up and press my face against the bars of the cell to actually see anything because he's pointing to the cell to the left of mine.

And what I see when I do that is… well… a very, very scary looking criminal. Another man, but this one looks nothing like either of the other two. He's leaning against the cinderblock wall with his arms crossed. And even though he's wearing a leather jacket with patches all over it, I can tell that he's very muscular. Under the jacket is a black concert t-shirt that looks like it's four decades old with a cracked and faded logo. And when my eyes travel down to where his happy trail would be, I find a thick leather belt and faded denim jeans. His head is shaved, and there's a cut across the side of his skull with dried blood all over it. His beard is dark and full, but neatly trimmed, and his piercing green eyes are looking at me like I'm naked.

My entire body shivers with desire as a feeling of absolute lust nearly knocks me over. And if there weren't steel bars blocking me, I would attack this man and start ripping his clothes off right here and now. I would grab him and tease him until he couldn't stand it anymore and had his way with me and—

I take a breath, actually startled at the salacious thoughts running through my head.

What the hell happened to me last night?

2 - ARIC

*D*eclan—that sneaky, ass-kissing, good-for-nothing Daddy's boy—points his finger at me from across the corridor while Quaid, Mr. Nobody himself, crosses his arms in satisfaction. Like they're a couple of children who just 'told' on me.

I'm leaning against the wall of my cell with my arms crossed, biding my time as these two cluelessly fumble their way through their first conversation with Star since she passed out last night.

Declan might be an ass kisser, but he's not ugly. He's a demigod, like me, but he's got that whole good-guy look to him. And while I might not know much about Star, I do know this—she would pick me over him every fucking day of the week. Let's just say that I am… her *type*.

She likes bad boys. At least, she does right now.

I nearly snicker as I remember using my power on her last night. There wasn't time to properly manipulate her—not with Declan and Mr. Nobody trying their best to interfere. But clearly my efforts were good enough to still be working this morning, because Star leans into the bars of her cell, trying her best to leer at me. And the moment she looks upon my demi-godly presence, her whole face goes kinda dreamy and sweet. She lets out a sigh, puckers her lips, and makes kissy noises at me.

Declan might be the son of Hermes, but his powers of persuasion won't break him out of that cell, now will it?

And as for Quaid, he's a worthless mortal. The only reason he was even in that bar last night was luck.

Luck and smooth-talking against *me*, son of Ares?

Come on.

The power I wield is almost unfair compared to those two losers. Magical artifact on my person aside, one inhale of my warrior scent was enough to turn her into a little slut. Seconds later, she was all over me. Clawing at my shirt, fingers fumbling with my belt, hand gripping my cock through my jeans. I was about to throw her down on the table and have my way with her when Mr. Nobody smashed a bottle over my head and broke the moment.

Then Declan was there, throwing punches.

The rest is, as they say, history.

Barroom brawl. My father would be proud.

But here in the mortal realm, I can't use my warrior blessings like I would in Olympus. And while I am a very strong warrior, it turns out that the bar was the off-duty hangout for every cop on the east side of Skyline City.

They descended on us like a swarm. I don't think they would've arrested Star if she hadn't been humping my leg while they were cuffing me, but I'm glad they did. At least I know where she is.

"Hey," I say, panning my arms wide. "What can I say? Getting people locked up is a talent of mine." This all comes out with a laugh.

Declan growls back at me. "Yeah, we know." Then rolls his eyes.

"Listen," I say, looking straight at Declan since those dark glasses of Quaid's always creep me out. "You know why I'm here. You both know why I'm here. I've got the claim of Ares and that trumps Hermes any day." I reluctantly shift my gaze to Quaid. "And don't even test me, mortal. You have no claim at all."

"You're wrong," Quaid says, sneering at me. "I've got the claim of Apollo."

"You can't claim anything for Apollo. You're a

nobody." Now I look at Declan. "The quicker we come to some kind of agreement here, the better."

Declan puts on his best charming smile. "You're high. I'm not here to negotiate. I told you that last night."

"What you're doing is none of my business, Declan. I'm here for her and, as you can see, she's not gonna put up a fight."

I lift up my hand and wave my fingers at Star, who is practically salivating over me now. "Hey there, darlin'. How ya feelin' this morning? Ready to rise and shine? Because I'm looking to get the fuck out of here pronto, and you're coming with me, right?"

She nods, still lost in her erotic dreams of my big dick. Which isn't a dream because she grabbed it last night. I bet she's thinking about that right now. How thick and hard it was. "I'm coming," she says, her voice nothing more than a soft whisper.

And my god, I'm nearly as turned on as she is. Before I hand her over to Ares, I'm gonna let her have her way with me. I won't even touch her. I'll make a vid, too. Just so I have proof that it was all her idea if Ares ever finds out.

"Star," Mr. Nobody says. "Look at me, babe. *Look at me!* Aric's done something to you. He's used some kind of curse on you and I need you to look at me so—"

"So you can *what?*" I interrupt. "You think you can break my curse? Or do you think she'll be more attracted to you than she is to *me?*"

"Star!" he says again. "Look at me!" And this time, his voice does something weird. It gets all deep and growly, echoing off the walls and shit. And while that's happening, those stupid sunglasses of his kinda flash or something.

And sure enough, when I look over at Star, she's looking at him and the curse has been broken. I know this because she's blinking real fast and, of course, this is not the first time I've used my powers to seduce a woman into seducing me, so I recognize the blinking.

"Hey," Declan says, elbowing Quaid. "What'd you do? How'd you counteract Aric, for fuck's sake? You're a nobody."

Even though I can't see Quaid's eyes behind those dumb sunglasses, I can tell they're narrowed because he's sneering when he side-eyes Declan. "How many fucking times do I have to spell it out for you people? I've been touched by Apollo. I have powers you can't even imagine."

Declan scoffs and I laugh.

Quaid thinks he's our equal?

That's actually funny.

"Quaid, you can counteract all you want. She'll never stop wanting me. Star," I say. And it comes out in a commanding voice, so she looks in my direction. Then, as she watches, I slide my hand down the front of my shirt, right down between my legs, and grab myself, giving my junk a tug to bring her eyes down where they need to be.

Sure enough, she blinks again.

Once more, she's under my curse.

3 - DECLAN

m I shocked that Quaid has hidden powers? Yes. Yes I am. But am I worried about it? Hell no. Like Aric said, he's nobody. A stupid mortal. Even if Star did choose to go with him over me, how far would they get? He can't take her to Olympus. Whatever touching Apollo has done to Quaid, it was on this side of things, not that one.

Plus, Star doesn't even remember who she is. And this memory hole goes far beyond what happened last night. I'm not exactly sure who she is either, but it doesn't matter. Aric was wrong about why I'm here. While I *was* sent here by my father, I'm not here to take Star back to him. I've been undercover, working for Hera, queen of the Gods, and I've got her blessing inside me. She gave me a boost of power that melds perfectly with my own—the ability to travel between worlds.

Quaid lives here in this realm, so I guess I can see him showing up at the last minute to ruin things. But Aric was a problem I didn't anticipate. Because he should not be here. Not even the son of Ares can walk through worlds. And he wasn't gifted with this power like I was. Hera said there was only one way for a demigod to make the journey—they must be able to carry information with them as they cross. Coordinates, as it turns out. But the message isn't the important part, it's the messenger. And that's me, son of Hermes. The most famous messenger of all time.

But the most pressing problem at the moment is that Aric has deployed an attraction curse on my Star and I don't understand how he's doing it. He shouldn't be able to affect her that way. Attraction against one's will isn't a blessing that might come from Ares, it's a curse which needs to be executed with an artifact. But he's not wearing any jewelry that I can see. Not even a watch.

All I know is that whatever is powering this curse is on his body somewhere, and I need to find it before he steals her away and ruins everything. Because if he can cross over to this side, then he must have a way to cross back as well.

He can't have her. Not ever. She's mine.

And I can prove it.

"Star, look at me." She doesn't, of course, because she's staring at Aric's dick. He's such a sick motherfucker. But in this instance, I don't need her eyes. I just need her ears…

"Da, da, dahhh, da, da, da, lies," I sing, using the melody we were working on last night, but inserting the word she just came up with. I have no clue what is up with this song, but it doesn't matter. My little Star is fixated on it and when I sing the melody, Aric's hold on her wavers.

His seduction curse weakens and Star looks in my direction as I sing the other part she came up with just before she was cursed by Aric. "Something, something, something, *eyes!*"

Star blinks, just like she did when Quaid broke Aric's hold over her, and stares at me.

"Damn you," Aric growls. "Stop fucking things up!"

I ignore him. Starting to panic. Because this is the extent of my knowledge about this stupid song. Which means it's my last chance to influence Star unless I get some more info. "Look at me, Star. You know the rest of the song, I know you do. Let's sing it now! Come on, dig deep into that brain of yours and tell me the rest of the words!"

"Don't listen to him, Star." This comes from Quaid. "If you give him those words, he'll cross back over to Olympus and he's gonna take you with him! Everyone you know on this side of things will be gone. Everything you have will be gone. *You'll be gone!* And there's no way back!"

I scoff at him. "That's not even true!"

"Star," Aric says, using that commanding voice again. "Look at me!"

"Don't," I yell. "Do not look at him! He's putting a curse on you, Star! To make you sexually want him! Don't you remember what you were doing last night when we got arrested? He had you humping his leg like a fucking dog!"

Aric's laugh is hearty. "You're jealous. Because that charm of yours is nothing compared to this." He pans his hand to his dick again. Which is now hard.

I make a face. "Gross, bru."

Poor Star. She looks like a deer in headlights. I wish I could just reach out and bring her into a great big hug. Mostly because that she wouldn't be able to look at Aric's dick or that weird flash in Quaid's eyes, but also because women like tenderness in a stressful situation.

I'm the tender one. That's me. Charming, easygoing Declan.

"Enough!" Star yells.

And suddenly, the whole place goes dark.

4 - QUAID

I stand still for a moment, wondering if Star's anger is a source of power that has thus far been left untapped and she's teleported us back to Olympus somehow, but no. It's not. Because the emergency lights flash on and a voice comes on the loudspeaker. "This is a test. Lights will be back on momentarily, lady and gentlemen. So don't get excited."

"Test?" Declan asks, looking at me. "Bullshit. Something's happening."

He's right. But I don't admit it. The insides of my sunglasses are lit up with data, and it's all I can do to keep up and make sense of it. Once the analysis is over, I withdraw inward so I can compile the information into something meaningful.

And then there it is. Meaning.

"Star," I say. My voice a little bit panicked. "We need to go." Immediately, Declan and Aric are protesting, each of them trying to get her to pay attention to them.

It's funny, in a way, how they think they are so powerful and us mortals are so weak. But they're standing inside mortal jail cells, desperately trying to siphon off Star's latent magic to find a way forward.

And me—Mr. Nobody, a pathetic mortal— can pop open these cells with my mind. I've already hacked into the sheriff's station security network. That *could* be why the lights went out. But if it is, it's a mistake. And I simply do not make mistakes.

So that's not the reason the lights went out.

The reason is Helix Order—a group of Titan worshipers who think Star is the key to unlocking the gates of Tartarus, where the Titans have been imprisoned for thousands of years. And while I have never studied their cult documents, nor do I understand their motives— anything that opens the door between the mortal realm and Tartarus is bad news. The Helix Order will do anything to get their claws on this key she has. And if they're close enough to be messing with the lights, they're moments away from obtaining their goal.

I need a plan.

The problem was never the jail cells. As soon as I took over the station network, I could've opened them up. That's no big deal.

But what I *can't do* is get us out of this building.

If Helix is outside, we can't get past them.

What we can do is…

Well, I hate to admit this, but Declan might be our only hope. As the demigod son of Hermes, he's got traveling gifts. And while I don't know for sure, I'm betting that means he could teleport us somewhere.

'Could' is the optimal word here. Because if it was that simple, he'd have done it already. And obviously, he's still here.

I turn to him. "Declan, can you get us out of here?"

His side-eye comes with a sneer. "Us?" Then a scoff. "Who the hell made you part of my crew?"

"Listen to me. We don't have much time. There's a mortal Titan cult called the Helix Order coming to get Star." I nod my head at her.

"What are you talking about?" Aric asks.

"None of your concern." I turn back to Declan. "They're here, Declan. And if we don't get out of here right now, they're gonna take Star. And I get it. We're all here to take Star. But they're different. What they do with her will be unconscionable. They'll torture her—"

"What?" Star is standing up, her hands wrapped around the bars of her cell, staring at us. "What did you just say?"

I ignore her and keep talking to Declan. "If you can get us out of here, you need to do it now!"

Declan laughs. "Like I said, Mr. Nobody. You're not one of us."

"Maybe not. But I'm betting the whole reason you haven't gotten yourself out of this jail in the first place is because you can't take Star with you. And the reason you can't take her with you is because you need to be touching her to do that and, obviously, we're in separate cells."

"So?" he says. "It's not like you've got any powers at all."

"Right," I laugh. "Well, what if I told you that I can open the cells?"

"Then do it, mortal." Aric hisses this at me.

I put up a hand. "You've got nothing to do with this, so—" But before I can finish my sentence, I hear gunshots from the other side of the jail door. "They're here! If you can get us out of the building, Declan, I'll open the cells."

"Open them!" Aric yells. "Open them and let me out!"

"Not you," I say again.

Just as Declan says, "OK. I'll do it."

I pop open our cell as well as Star's, and we all rush out, reaching for each other.

But the moment I touch Declan, and Declan touches Star—*she touches Aric.*

And we all disappear together.

5 - STAR

My eyes are bouncing back and forth between the three men as they argue about getting out of here. As if breaking out of jail is just something one does when they wake up there after a night gone wrong.

So I'm mostly concentrating on this, and not that fact that the cell doors actually pop open when it happens. But when Happy Trail Declan comes rushing at me, parts of their conversation start to make sense.

Whatever is going on here, he and Sunglasses are leaving and they're taking me with them.

I don't know why I reach over and touch Aric's arm once I'm outside the cell. All I know is that I felt compelled to do it.

And now that we're… somewhere else. Some place that is not a jail cell. I'm suddenly very glad he's here. Because those two guys were in the middle of *kidnapping me*! And while I don't know a damn thing about the one called Aric other than he's got a giant snake of a dick inside those tight jeans of his, I understand that he's not friends with them.

Perhaps the shaved-headed biker isn't the best person to pin my hopes on when it comes to saving me from kidnappers, but he's all I've got.

And the instant I touch him, both Declan and Quaid touch me, and then we are...

Well. Nowhere. *Total darkness.*

"Where the hell are we?" Aric bellows. "What the hell did you do?"

"Is everybody OK?" Quaid asks. Suddenly, a hand is grabbing me. "Star? Is that you?"

"Don't touch me," I say, brushing his hand away. "I don't even know you! And I want to know the same thing! Where the hell are we? I mean, this isn't normal! One minute I'm safe inside a jail cell and the next thing I know, I'm literally standing in the middle of nothingness."

"It's OK, Star." Suddenly Aric is next to me. "I won't let them hurt you."

"Oh, will you give it a rest?" Quaid barks back. "Quit acting like you're some kind of good guy."

"Well, at least I didn't just snatch her away from the mortal world and drop her ass off in the pits of Hell."

"*What?*" I say. And it's not a calm outburst, either. It's actually rather shrieky. "Did he just say pits of Hell?"

"Obviously, it's not the pits of Hell," Quaid says. "And for your information, Mr. Motorcycle, this is still the mortal realm."

"How would you know?" Aric snaps back. "You're Mr. Nobody."

"You keep saying that, and yet I was the one—"

"Wait!" I say, interrupting their argument. "Where's the other guy?"

"Declan?" Quaid asks. "He's right—" But he doesn't finish. And even in the dark, I can tell he's looking for him. Reaching blindly through the air. I know this because his hand bumps in to me, right across my breast.

"Hey!" I say.

"Oh, that's you, sorry."

"You just grabbed me!"

"What?" Aric growls.

"I didn't!" Quaid says. "I was looking for Declan! Clearly, he is missing."

"How could he be missing?" I ask. "I mean, I don't actually understand what just happened back there, but I'm not stupid and I'm pretty sure he's the one who got us out of the jail."

"No," Quaid protests. "*I* was the one who got us out of the jail cell. He just took us… well. I'm not sure."

Aric huffs. "That little brown-nosing asshole had better not be missing. I'm not getting stuck in the pits of Hell."

"We're not in the pits of Hell," Quaid says. "How many times do I have to say it?"

"Declan!" I call. "Are you here?"

"If he was here," Aric growls at *me* now. "He would be talking. Trust me, that guy never shuts up."

"We need to find him," I say. "Like right now. I'm not getting stuck in the pits of Hell, either."

"Oh, my god," Quaid says. His tone filled with exasperation. "How many times—"

But I don't hear the rest because I trip over something and fall on my face. Except, my face doesn't hit the hard ground, because my hands fly out in front of me and break my fall.

Except they don't hit the hard ground, either. They hit... a body.

A very muscular and cut chest on a body. And I know this is Declan because my face lands right over top of that perfect blond happy train. I'm talking right on top of it. I could pop the button on his jeans with my teeth.

"Declan?" I say. "Oh, my god, I think he's dead. I just fell on him!"

Both of the guys shuffle through the darkness until they're close enough to bend down. Meanwhile, I have pulled myself up—reluctantly

—and I'm straddling Declan's thighs as my hands caress his perfect abs.

I gasp and pull them back. Feeling slightly ashamed at myself since he's probably unconscious, but also slightly grossed out since he could be dead.

"Is he breathing?" Quaid asks.

"I don't know!" I say. "But he better be! He's our only way back!" Then I have a brilliant idea. A sexy, perfect, so-in-the-moment brilliant idea, I don't even discuss it with the other two guys before I put it into action.

He needs mouth to mouth.

I reach up, place my hands flat on his face, and then lean down and kiss him. I mean, I blow lifesaving oxygen into his airway. Except, I don't. I *actually* kiss him. And even though he's unconscious and might even be dead, the shame and disgust are gone and in their place is… bliss.

Pure bliss.

Like Declan, the total stranger, messenger guy with the hot body, is my one true love.

6 - ARIC

Star is kissing him! It takes me a moment to figure out what's happening, and this is way too long to stop what comes next. But she's not just kissing him, she's grinding on him. Like he's got some kind of hold over her!

Which I need to put a stop to immediately.

Fuck that. His gifts are charm and moving through worlds. I'm the fucking sex god here.

Demigod, technically. But that's my kiss, not his! I'm the one with the belt buckle. It's holding the curse of attraction that Ares gave me to be used in exactly this kind of situation.

And Declan has the nerve to steal this moment from me?

No.

I pull her back, hook my arms under hers, and drag her away.

"What is going on?" Quaid asks. "Was she just kissing him?"

"Yes. He put some kind of curse on her and—"

Star begins to kick and scram. "Get off me! Let me go! I need to give him mouth to mouth!"

"Mouth to mouth?" Quaid sneers.

And just as he says that, Declan starts laughing. "I did it! I got the first kiss! She's mine now! Rules are rules!"

"Rules?" Quaid asks. He's such a Mr. Nobody. He doesn't even understand that in the world of demigods, the first kiss is the claim. "What the hell kind of game are you two playing?"

"Star," I say, pulling her to her feet and shaking her a little. "Snap out of it! Look at me!" But while I'm saying this, I'm unbuckling my belt.

"Bro," Quaid says, flicking a lighter on so he can see. "Did you just unbuckle your belt? What the hell is happening here? Have you two freaks lost your minds?"

Star is still struggling while Declan gets to his feet. "Let her go, Aric. You saw it. She kissed me first. She's mine."

This makes Star go still, but I don't let go of her. She takes a breath and composes herself. "Did you just trick me?"

"Yep," I say. "He did. Which means, it doesn't count. And anyway—" I have my belt off now, but it's only the buckle holding the curse of attraction that I need. "Star has already been claimed by *me*!" Then I shove the belt buckle up to her face. And thanks to Quaid's lighter, she sees it. And in this moment, she blinks. When the blink is over, her eyes find mine and they are filled with lust.

"That's right," I say. "See?" I lean in to her, pushing my face up to hers like we're about to take a selfie together. "We're a couple now. She was mine first, Declan and—"

But suddenly I am thrown backwards, and the darkness is back. Because Quaid drops the lighter when he attacks me.

"You freak! Both of you," Quaid says. He grabs the collar of my leather jacket and slams me into a rock wall. Then he pulls Star out of my reach. "Get away from us! The two of you are sick! She's not a prize, for fuck's sake! She's a woman!"

The lighter flicks on again, only this time, Declan's the one holding it. "Listen, Quaid. While I do appreciate your help back there in the cell, this is none of your business. You're the one who needs to back off. This is between me and Aric."

"Fuck that," Quaid says, still backing up. "I'm not leaving her with you freaks."

"Bru," I say. Remaining remarkably calm. But that's only because he's Mr. Nobody. He's got no chance of claiming Star, so I'm not even worried about it. I cursed her first. Declan's kiss doesn't count. She's mine and that's the end of it. "Just let her go and then you can be on your way and we'll take it from here."

"The hell you will," Quaid snaps. He's still backing up. And then, right before our eyes, they both just… vanish.

Like into thin air.

7 - DECLAN

I blink my eyes. Then blink them again. "Where the hell did they go?" I spin in place, holding the lighter up, looking all around. But all I see is a gray wall of smooth stone. "Aric!" I yell.

"I'm right here, bru. You don't need to scream like a little bitch."

I whirl around and find him on the ground, holding his head.

"Why are you just sitting there on the ground like a lazy fuck? They just disappeared!"

He gets to his feet. "No shit. I was here, remember?"

"Why were you on the ground?"

"Something..." He sighs. Then takes a breath. "Something... knocked me over."

"What do you mean, *something*? What are you talking about?"

"I..." He looks around, his eyes all narrowed in suspicion. "I don't know."

"Was it Quaid?"

Aric looks in the direction where Quaid was, then shakes his head. "No. It wasn't Quaid. I saw them disappear, then everything went dark—"

"Yeah, the lighter was burning my thumb."

"Well, when everything went dark something... hit me." He looks at me now. And this look is, well, it's not fear. Not exactly. But it's definitely concern. "It hit me *hard*, too." He puts a flat hand on the middle of his chest. "Right here. Knocked the fuckin' wind out of me."

"What are you talking about? What kind of something?"

He looks around again. "I'm not sure." And now he's whispering.

Which, not gonna lie, concerns me. So I hold the lighter up and look around as well. "What is this place?"

Aric doesn't answer, just keeps slowly spinning, like he's expecting an attack.

I sniff the air. "What is that stench? Is that you?"

Aric shoots me a look, offended. "Shut the fuck up, would you? Do you want it to attack again?"

"It? What is this 'it' you say attacked you?

Because I didn't experience an attack and I was standing right here."

But he's not looking at me. And he doesn't keep the argument going. Which also concerns me, because in my experience, a good-natured argument is a nice way to defuse a stressful situation and someone who is sharing that stressful situation with you should appreciate this.

"Give me that lighter." Aric grabs for it, but I pull it back.

"Get your own fuckin' lighter."

He stares at me, his eyes blazing with anger now. "What are you, fourteen? Give me the fuckin' lighter!" Then he just snatches it out of my hand, flicks it back on, and starts walking.

"Where are you going?"

"Look," he says, pointing into the darkness. "It's a… hallway. Or maybe…" He looks up and around. "A tunnel, maybe."

I look up and around too. "A tunnel? Why the hell would we be in a tunnel?"

"I have no fuckin' idea," Aric sneers. "I'm not the one who brought us here. You are."

Which is true, so I don't really have a comeback for that.

"Look," he says. Again, pointing towards the darkness. "There's an opening over there."

"Who cares! What we need to do is find Mr. Nobody and Star!"

He ignores me and walks forward, leaving me in the darkness because he takes our only source of light with him. So of course, I have to follow.

He stops, waving the lighter around, trying to see everything. "What's all this?" he asks.

I squint and lean in to see what he's pointing at. There are little markings all over the smooth gray stones that make up the wall. "Looks like symbols, or something."

Aric whirls around, sniffing the air. "Oh. Fuck."

I whirl too—unsure what I'm looking for. "Oh, fuck, what?"

"That smell... I know that smell."

"What are you talking about?"

"Oh, shit," he says, walking forward again. "Oh, fuck."

"Bru!" I say. "What is happening?"

He turns and his face has gone completely white. "I know where we are."

I wait, but he doesn't say anything. "Well? Where the fuck are we!"

He opens his mouth to answer, but instead of hearing words, I hear a sort of... snarling? Sniffing? Snorting?

Aric turns and then yells, "*Ruuun!*"

I've never claimed to be the smartest of men. I mean, look at me. When you're blessed with this body and face—not to mention the hair— brains are really just an accessory. But when a demigod tells me to run in a voice that suggests this action will save my life, I'm all instinct.

Aric takes off and I'm done asking questions, I am right behind him.

But there's something right behind *me*.

Hooves. It sounds like hooves. Not some happy clip-cloppy sound of a horse on a hack being ridden by one of those English girls who wear all those sexy horse-riding outfits, either. More like the sound of hooves when a monster is at your back and any moment now, it's gonna grab you with a clawed hand and rip you to pieces.

"What the fuck!" I yell. "What the fuck is happening?" This is when I overtake Aric. I mean, I am the son of Hermes. The whole 'wings on his feet' might just be a metaphor, but the speed is real, not to mention genetic, so I'm quick as fuck.

But he's got the lighter, so I can't see where I'm going until a wall is nearly in my face. I almost smash into it, barely turning in time, only to find myself presented with another wall!

"This place is like a maze!" I yell.

"No shit," Aric yells. "That's because it *is* a maze! It's the fuckin' Labyrinth! And that thing chasing us is the Minotaur!"

None of these words makes sense. There's no Labyrinth. There's no Minotaur. That shit was taken care of a decade back. But just as these words are forming in my head, Aric says, "Watch out!"

Which makes me stumble, allowing him to pass me, and then a burning across my back, the likes of which I've never felt before, makes me fall forward onto my knees.

I quickly scramble, turning my body around to face the oncoming threat and when I look up, I'm staring straight into the glowing red eyes of a monster that shouldn't exist!

8 - QUAID

When I grab Star's arm, three things happen at once.

First—the world blinks and everything—including Star and me—turns into nothing but a teal green outline.

Second—the lighter flicks off, so everything around Declan and Aric, goes dark.

And third—the space in front of Aric goes... blurry, or something. And he goes flying backwards, landing on his ass.

Then, Star screams.

Out of instinct, I clamp a hand over her mouth, because that blur disappears again, but not before I get a glimpse of *horns*.

I pull her to my chest and walk backwards, melding right into the wall and removing us both from the situation.

Then I whirl her around—everything about her outlined in teal green—and deactivate the tech inside my glasses. Her eyes are wide with surprise, looking at me like I'm a freak. Because the world is not supposed to be nothing but a glowing outline. But it only takes a moment for that to disappear and for us to become 'real' again.

She opens her mouth to scream, but I clamp my hand over it again and shake my head. Then I whisper, "Don't make a sound. We're out of immediate danger, but if we landed where I think we did, it won't be safe for long. Do you understand me?"

She doesn't move. Doesn't even blink.

"Star!" I whisper yell, kind of shaking her at the same time. "Do you understand?"

I get a nod this time.

"Good. I'm gonna take my hand away from your mouth and you're gonna remain silent and still." Slowly, I remove my hand.

And immediately, she's broken her word! "What the hell! What the fuck?"

"Shhhh," I say. Very insistent now. "We're in a lot of danger and—"

But my words are broken by a scream somewhere else in the maze.

Star whirls around, looking in all directions in the dark. "What the fuck was that?"

I sigh. "Declan, I think."

"*What?*" Now she's looking at me again.

"Don't worry. He's a demigod. He'll pull through."

Star grabs me by the collar and starts shaking me. "What the fuck is going on!"

I grab her wrists and hold them tight. "I get it, it's confusing. You lost your memory. You have no idea who you are. And the three of us all showing up on the same night—well, it's a lot. So I get it. But you need to calm the fuck down and listen to me. Because both of those men back there, they claimed you. I don't know how Aric did it, but Declan did it with that trick of a kiss and—"

"*Kiss?*" She's hysterical. "Who the hell cares about a stupid kiss! Three seconds ago, I was a glowing green outline! We... you... I went through a wall! A wall, Mr. Nobody! A fucking wall!"

I push her away from me, kinda hard, too. "Don't call me that! I was the one who saved your ass! Twice!"

She stares at me, stunned by my angry outburst.

Which affords me the opportunity to take a breath and get myself under control. "I'm just gonna spell it out for you, OK? Because you're clearly in a state."

She puts her hands on her hips. "A *state?*"

"You're not who you think you are. You're

not even mortal. This life you're living? It's all a lie. You were sent here to the mortal world because you're a lynchpin in an ancient Titan prophecy."

"You're insane! Get away from me!" She turns and tries to run, but I quickly lean forward, grab her around the waist, and push her up against a wall. Immediately, she and I are struggling, but she's very small and I'm *not*, so she's got no chance at all.

"*Listen*," I say. Kinda shoving her into the wall a little. This one word comes out way too strong, and in combination with the shoving, scares her. So she recoils. "Your real name is Pleiades Eight, not Star. You're the missing Sister. Daughter of the sea nymph, Pleione, and King Aegeus. You were hidden away by Hera upon your birth to prevent a prophecy from coming true."

"*What?*"

"You don't remember because Hera wiped your memory. You're some kind of keystone in the return of the Titans. Somehow, some way, you help them escape from their eternal prison in Tartarus. Naturally, this is a very bad idea. Hera didn't want to kill you outright—she wasn't sure what kind of power you might wield. So instead, she sent you to live in the mortal world."

"You're crazy! All that stuff is just myth! And anyway, it happened thousands of years ago!"

"No. It's clearly not a myth because you were

imprisoned with two demigods just ten minutes ago. They were both sent to retrieve you. Don't ask me why, I don't know. All I know is that they can't have you."

"So *you* took me." She's furious now. But at least she's listening.

"Yes. I was sent by Apollo."

"So you want me as well?"

"Of course. Everyone wants you, Star. You're the key to everything. But we've got a serious problem."

"No shit. We're in some kind of maze. I might not be a history expert, but from my recollection, the Labyrinth is the home of a monster and everyone sent inside is eaten by it!"

"Not exactly. And, this isn't the real Labyrinth, obviously. Your half-brother killed the Minotaur about a decade back. Olympus is not a myth. It's just another dimension. They live on a similar timeline, so it's all happening at the same time. This world, that world, it's all connected. Declan is the son of Hermes, messenger to the Gods. A traveler. That's how he passed through the worlds. That's how he got us out of the sheriff's station. Aric is the son of Ares. And trust me when I say this, that guy is bad. Ares is the God of War. He's a savage brute and it would be a huge mistake to assume his son is any different. I don't know how Aric got here. What I do know is that he put a seduction curse on you to make you want him. That's why you were throwing yourself at him last night. And Declan, he got you to kiss him back there. I don't know what the rules are about kissing, but if what he said was true, and it's a claim, then we've got a huge problem."

She's tapping her toe, her arms crossed over her chest. "Let me guess. You have to claim me too."

I point at her and smile. "That's correct. If I claim you now, they can't take you and—"

"What makes you think I don't want to be taken?"

"Well," I laugh. "Excuse me for assuming you didn't want to be used as a pawn in a war between the Olympians and the Titans. My bad."

She goes silent for a moment. Then, finally says, "What does your claim involve?"

I nearly grin, only barely managing to tuck it down. "Just a little piece of jewelry."

"Let me see it."

I reach into my coat pocket and pull out the bit of leather and silver.

Star squints. "Is that a..." She leans in. Then looks up at me. "Is that a *collar*?"

I press my lips together and nod. "It is. It's not just any collar, though. It's connected to these." I point to my sunglasses. "Which are connected to Apollo."

"Who you work for."

"Correct."

"And he's the god of…?"

"Oh, hell. That guy can do just about anything. But mainly, as it pertains to you, he's in charge of your prophecy."

She taps her toe again. "I see." Hands on hips again. "Well. Isn't that convenient."

She's not gonna let me put this collar on. I can see the argument coming. But this is not a choice, and she's not in charge here, I am.

Our eyes are locked when these thoughts go through my head and it's like she's reading my mind, because she turns to run.

But I simply change us back into the in-between state of glowing green outlines, confusing her long enough to slip the collar around her neck and seal it forever with the magic of Apollo.

9 - STAR

The moment his collar clamps tight around my neck, I feel a surge of energy. Something powerful and shocking at the same time. A jolt electrifies me and suddenly the whole world turns into a glowing teal-green outline. The effect is different this time. I get dizzy, and my heart starts racing, and my mind is spinning because what I'm looking at isn't possible. I laugh. "I can see through walls!"

"Fuck!" Quaid says. He starts tapping on his sunglasses. "What the fuck did you just do?"

I sneer at him. "What did *I* do? I didn't do anything. You're the one who wanted to put this stupid collar on me!" I grab at it, trying to find the clasp so I can take it off, but there is no clasp. It's just leather with silver embellishments all the way around. "Take it off," I say. "Take it off right now!"

Quaid reaches for the piece of jewelry around my neck, scoffing. "Gladly. You're a mistake, that's all you are. I'm not sure why Apollo thought you were so important, but you're obviously not. You're just a bit of interference."

I flip a hand at him. "Whatever. Just take it off."

"I'm trying," he says. "I can't find the clasp."

"That's because there is no clasp. I don't know what kind of magic, or whatever, you used to put it on, but do that in reverse right now, *please.*"

"I didn't do any magic. It's not magic. It's science."

"Again. Whatever. Just take it off!"

"I can't." He slips his fingers underneath the leather and they're sliding around my neck. This sends shivers up my spine and suddenly, the world blinks.

"Stop it," he says.

"I didn't do anything. Why is this thing still on me? Get it *off.*"

"I'm dead serious here, Star. Whatever little game you're playing with my sunglasses, stop it right now. You're fucking up the program."

"I'm not doing anything." But he's touching me again, moving my hair out of the way to get a better look at the collar and he's very close. So close, his warm breath is right against my ear. Another shiver goes up my spine, making my skin prickle up.

The world around us glitches again, but this time, some of it disappears. Which is kind of a good thing because when the whole world is nothing but green outlines, it's very hard to make sense of that.

But when all the closest outlines flick off, I can suddenly see very, very far. Literally, looking through walls. Hurriedly, I scan around, searching for Declan. If that really was him screaming, he's in a lot of danger.

There's a flash of movement far off in the black distance. I can't really make anything out, but I know in my heart, that's where Declan is. I point in that direction. "We need to go over there, Quaid. Right now! Before anything bad happens to Declan!"

"Fuck Declan," Quaid mutters under his breath. Which shoots right up my neck, and in this same moment, his fingertips thread up into my hair in the same place. A sudden spark of arousal shoots through me, and the outline flickers off.

"Dammit, Star! What did you just do?"

"Stop blaming everything on me! This is all your fault. You're the one who put—"

"Don't move." He jerks me towards him. "I'm trying to figure this out." Then grabs my hip, pulling me closer to him. And at the same time, the world flicks on again. "See," he sneers. "I told you it was you. You're doing all of this."

I scoff. But don't continue the argument, because there's a lot of movement over in the distance again. "Quaid! We need to go over there, now!" I take a step forward, but this time he wraps one arm all the way around my waist, encircling me in a light grip.

He grabs my shoulders, turns me around, and leans way down into my personal space so that I'm looking right into his sunglasses. "How many times do I have to tell you, *stay still!*"

There's light in there, so I get preoccupied with it. I can see his eyes through the dark lenses and they're *glowing*. I stare right into them and suddenly, they get brighter.

Then I notice that he's breathing a little heavy. His hands come up to my face, one on each cheek and we stay like this for what seems like a very long time, but probably just a few seconds.

Suddenly the sunglasses light up with a bright flash. So bright, I have to close my eyes, and even then, the residual flash remains on the inside of my eyelids.

But the really weird thing is, when I open them again, I'm looking down at my own face.

"What the fuck, Star!"

And these words, though they are not mine,

they're his—in his voice and everything—I feel like they are coming out of my own mouth.

"Get out of my head!" He pushes me away and whatever was happening, it abruptly stops and I'm me again.

I'm breathless when I speak. "What the hell was that?"

"You were inside me! I don't know what you think you're doing, but—"

But I'm not listening. I'm repeating his words back in my head. *You were inside me.*

I was! I really, really was.

But the funny thing is, I think I... *liked it.*

I felt his power. Not just whatever magic those sunglasses are doing, though I did feel that too, but his power. The power of being him. Quaid, the man.

And honestly, it's kinda sexy.

Not me being him.

Him. Just him.

Immediately, I'm aroused. I'm talking... all the way around kind of aroused. The throbbing between my legs is like a tiny pulse of electricity.

The world glitches again, and then it's back. I'm in his head. This time though, I don't waste it. I look over at the spot where I saw the movement a few minutes ago, and then Quaid wrestles back the power of his glasses from me and I start running.

Right through the walls. Or, where they would be, if they were here.

"No!" Quaid yells. "Stop right now! You're fucking up the software!"

But I don't stop because just a few paces in, I see Declan and the monster attacking him and I run harder, a straight line through all the invisible walls of the maze, heading right towards it.

Quaid grabs me by the arm and pulls me back with such force, we both fall to the ground, and the moment we hit, the walls are back.

And when I look at Quaid, his sunglasses are no longer black and all I see are bright green eyes staring back at me.

Powerless, bright green eyes.

He growls. And it's a real one. I know, because his lip actually goes up into a sneering snarl over his teeth. "Congratulations, you fucking brat." Those green eyes narrow down into tiny slits. "We're all gonna die because of you."

I slowly raise my middle finger at him.

And then I get up and I *run*.

10 - ARIC

I turn back in the stone hallway and find the claws of my worst nightmare snatching Declan and pulling backwards so hard, when he slams on the ground, I am a hundred percent sure he's dead.

The only reason I don't freak out about this is because he's a demigod, like me, and it'll take much more than that to kill him.

I am a hundred-and-one percent sure of this fact. Because this isn't just any maze or any monster, this is *my* maze. *My* monster.

My training grounds, to be exact.

When I was sixteen, my father made this maze so he could turn me into a soldier. I can still see, with perfect clarity, that look in his eyes when he brought me here for the first time.

"You're weak," he said. His words coming out

like venom. "You're pathetic. And if you can't live up to my name, Aric, then you don't deserve to live at all."

I was never a small boy. How could I be? I was Ares's bastard son and took after him in build and muscle. So these insults weren't based in facts. They were never meant to physically describe me, they were meant to emotionally hurt me.

Because pain, in the eyes of Ares, builds character. And character builds heroes. And if I wasn't gonna grow up to be a hero, he didn't want me around.

He was training me to be a warrior and the only way to cure fear is to face all the consequences of losing before you ever step out onto the battlefield.

That's what this maze was. My battlefield.

The day he brought me here was my sixteenth birthday.

The next time I saw daylight, I was twenty-one.

Five years.

He left me here to fight this monster in the maze for five fucking years.

It's not real, this place. Well, it is, in every way that matters. But it's not Olympus and it's not the mortal realm either. It's something in between.

Some kind of illusion.

If an illusion could literally decapitate you, and you don't die. Just wake up in your bed like it never happened.

Except it did happen and there was no way to forget.

I died every way possible.

I suffered every pain imaginable at the hands of this monster.

And I came out the other side with every single memory intact.

This is how you build character, my father told me.

This is how you make a warrior.

I've never been the same since.

So when I see my nightmare pulling Declan away with those massive claws, I freeze. I can't process what I'm seeing. I killed it, even though it wasn't really alive, it bled. I took its head off. I cut it up into little pieces and threw them into the fire. I watched it burn, bit by bit. I ground those horns down into dust with a crude grindstone. So that when I left this place, I knew I would never have to come back because the monster was gone.

And yet, here it is.

My monster. Doing its best to kill Declan right in front of my eyes.

I can't move. I'm frozen, like I looked the Medusa in the eyes and was turned to rock.

I went crazy in here.

Lost my fucking mind.

Was talking to myself.

Making up rhymes to pass the time because I lost my mind.

Suddenly, I hear Star screaming Declan's name. Then pounding footsteps. From around a corner she appears, Quaid following behind her.

The spell the maze cast over me, fades and I blink. Just like Star blinked back in the jail cell.

She stops dead, then begins to scream.

And the words—the crazy rambling of the boy I was, but will never be again—start coming back to me.

Quaid pushes Star out of the way, shoving her behind him.

And this is it. My time to shine in the grand design.

I move, straight at the Minotaur, and just before it swipes another claw over Declan's body on the ground, I grab him. Picking him up with all the strength of the man I am.

I take him with me, heading straight towards Star, the words already spilling out of my mouth, unbidden, but there, nonetheless.

"Midnight dreams and moonlit lies."

Star's eyes go wide with surprise!

"The fates of three and one collide."

Fuck this place, I will not die.

"Charm to ease your growing fear. Strength

to let the brightness near. A final gift to be your eyes." And then I yell, "*Ruuuuun!*"

Quaid grabs Star, following me and then, the impossible happens.

The world blinks, the walls disappear, and we go right through them.

11 - DECLAN

I'm having the strangest experience. Painful, but overall, not entirely bad. I'm standing up, but looking down at my own body at the same time. Like I'm having one of those out-of-body experiences.

Near death. That's the state I'm in. I've been here before, so it's kinda familiar. And it makes sense because I was attacked by a monster. But it also doesn't make sense because... I was attacked by a monster.

Where the fuck am I?

I turn in place, looking around, but it's actually not that easy to describe this room.

It's... a bar? No. A bedroom? Not quite. A strip club? Getting closer.

It's a weird mash-up of all three of those things. Of course, the three strippers are holograms. They're dancing inside cages that flicker and glitch, like the program running them is old and out of date. They're all naked so I watch them slowly gyrate against the bars of their cages to a bluesy song for a moment, as Aric, Quaid, and Star look down at my seemingly lifeless body on the ground with worried eyes.

What a strange room. I'm still trying to make sense of it when this statement comes right out of Quaid's mouth. "What a weird room. I can't tell if this is a brothel or a night club. What the hell is this place?"

Star snickers. "Yeah, it's like we were dropped into the fantasy of a fourteen-year-old boy."

Aric stiffens, straightening up. "I was sixteen, OK. This was my only safe place in the entire maze so I made my own. Excuse me if my décor is not up to your standards."

Quaid laughs. "What?" He looks at Star. "What did he just say?"

Star just glares at Quaid, not answering.

So Aric continues. "This." He points to the ground. "Is my home base."

"Your what?" Quaid chuckles.

"My base, you fuckwit. In the Labyrinth. These hallways and passages were my training grounds. It was how Ares turned me into a warrior. It was how he turned me into a man."

Star is frowning. She straightens up too and

now no one is even paying attention to my nearly lifeless body on the ground. She says, "I don't understand."

"You wouldn't, would you?" Surprisingly, this doesn't come from Aric, but Quaid. And he's sneering at her. Like she repulses him. "Why would you understand any of this? You're some hidden-away Pleiades princess living out your cushy life in the mortal realm under the protection of Hera." His disgust is so obvious now, it's getting weird. "You don't know anything."

Aric steps in front of Star, cutting off Quaid's view of her. "What's your problem?"

Quaid runs fingers through his hair, looking away. "Nothing."

"I'll tell you what his problem is," Star peeks out from behind Aric. "His problem is, he can't control me. Not even with the collar around my neck."

Aric, like me, must take a moment to put all the pieces together, because he goes silent. Quaid, Mr. Nobody who works for Apollo, put a *collar* on Star. Why? I mean, collars imply possession and control, so I guess that's not hard to figure out. But why would he need that control?

Hmm. Mr. Nobody, who seems to be in possession of some very magical sunglasses, came here with a directive.

Which isn't a surprise, didn't we all come here to get Star and take her back to someone?

We did.

But neither Aric nor myself are invested in the task.

It's a job to us. I would not say kidnapping a hidden princess from the mortal realm is a regularly occurring request as a bounty hunter, but it's on the list of services. At least at my office. I don't know what kind of bounty hunter business Aric runs. For all I know, he only works for his father. Which kinda makes sense, now that I think about it. Ares is giving off greedy, controlling, selfish vibes and he's not even here in the room with us.

Quaid is different. He's not a demigod and he doesn't live in Olympus. He's a… well, employee is probably the nicest word to describe him, but slave is the most likely answer.

Unless he's got some breeding on his pedigree that I don't know about, he shouldn't be in possession of glasses that have hidden powers. Gods, especially very powerful, high-ranking ones like Apollo, don't just hand over magic sunglasses to mortals.

Again, Aric and I are on the same page, because just as I think this, he points to Quaid and says, "She's your ticket, isn't she?"

Quaid doesn't say anything. Just shoves his hands in his pockets.

So Aric continues, practically reading my mind. "You made a deal with Apollo." Aric's eyes go squinty, as do mine, as we both work out the next piece of the puzzle. "What is she worth to you, Quaid? Hm? A one-way ticket into Olympus? A get-out-of-slavery-free card? What did Apollo promise you if you brought him Star?"

Quaid maintains his very detached, cool demeanor. "Well, I guess it doesn't matter anymore. The glasses are broken. They don't work. So I hope you have a way out of your teenage-wet-dream room, because I sure don't."

I think I want to wake up now.

I want to participate in this exchange because there's something happening here that needs to be worked out. But when I step over to my body on the ground, I don't go back in.

It's not ready for me. That monster must be very powerful if it affected me this way. And I guess it would have to be, if Ares's goal was to turn his son into a warrior. The monster should be formidable and hard to kill. Ares would want the consequences to be severe enough to shape Aric, should he ever fail.

I guess that's why he's such a dick.

I can't die, not easily. Decapitation would do it. But even then, under extenuating circumstances, I could technically be put back together. My messenger stage—this ghost form that I'm in now—is supposed to be transient. A blip of time—or, more accurately, no-time—in which I move through space. That's how I get places so fast.

I'm not the messenger of the gods, that's my father, Hermes. But the gift of travel was inherited, nonetheless. And now, it seems, I am stuck in this state. Already out of the game and I didn't even know I was playing.

Aric has been staring at Quaid this whole time I was thinking, and now he lets out a breath. "I'm gonna let this go," he says, "but it's not over. I will figure out what you're up to, Quaid. But right now, I'd rather focus all my attention on getting the hell out of here without having to run this maze ten-thousand times before we kill the monster. Because that's the only way out that I know of. And Declan here isn't gonna be any help until he heals himself, obviously. So instead of standing there looking like a surly asshole, why don't you come up with some ideas."

Before Quaid can answer, Star steps out from behind Aric. "No." She looks manic. "I'm not listening to his ideas and even if he came up with one, I'm not going anywhere with him!"

She starts this sentence angry, but she ends it absolutely furious. So furious, she gives off a powerful energy and three things happen at once.

First, the room brightens, then goes completely dark.

Second, Quaid's sunglasses also go bright, but then they go black and start to glow a bright teal-green color.

And third, the walls all come to life. All those little symbols that Aric and I saw carved into the walls are now glowing with white light. Some of the symbols I recognize from the academy I went to as a kid. We had to learn all kinds of ancient languages. But some of them are very strange and I have no idea what they mean.

It doesn't matter, though, because the point is, they're saying *something*.

Except, I don't think anyone else can see this but me, because the lights are back on now, and both Aric and Quaid are discussing what just happened to his stupid sunglasses and aren't saying anything at all about the walls.

Aric points to Star. This is when I start paying attention again. "It's you," he says.

She points to herself. "What's me?"

"You're the one making his glasses glitch like that."

"So?" She's very defensive.

"It's not exactly her," Quaid says. "I've already figured this out."

"Then why didn't you say anything?" Aric asks.

He sneers at Star. "Because she's not gonna like what I have to say."

A moment of silence hangs after these words come out, and in this same moment my body must have repaired itself enough to pull me back in, because the next thing I know, I'm on the ground, sitting up.

It's me who puts the last piece of the puzzle together. "She's can power them." Everyone looks down at me.

Star smiles. "You're OK!"

"I'm OK."

Aric offers me his hand. I take it, and he pulls me to my feet. "What were you saying now?"

I point at Star. "Her hidden magic. I think you unlocked it."

"Unlocked it how?" Quaid asks. "Aric didn't do anything but bring us to this ridiculous room filled with holographic strippers. I'm the one who put the collar on her."

"You're wrong," I say. "He did something very important." I point at Star again. "He knew your song. He said the words. And that's all you needed to hear to come into your true power."

Quaid almost snorts. "So what? You're missing the point, Declan. Who cares about the song?" He looks at Aric. "You wanna know why I'm here?" He pans his arms wide, motioning to Star. "There is it. She's a power source and Apollo wants to add her to his collection."

"What are you talking about?" I ask.

"How do you think he got so powerful, Declan? Come on, use those two brain cells inside your head. He steals it. Star is just one of many astral maidens who can control the movement of the constellations." He reluctantly looks at Star and shrugs. "It's kind of a big deal. That's why it brought my glasses back online."

"I don't understand," Star says. "How did I do that?"

"Emotions," Quaid says. "You got emotional and it affected the tech inside the glasses. That's not the only way to manifest your power, but exciting you is the easiest way." Now he looks at me and Aric. "If we can work her up a little, maybe I can get enough time to run a diagnostic and fix them. And if I can fix them," he locks eyes with me. "I can travel and take everyone with me."

I shrug. "So. I can do that too."

"So do it," Aric says. "Get us the fuck out of here."

Star rushes up to me, grabbing my arm, like I might leave her behind and she's gonna make sure that doesn't happen. And I notice, out of the corner of my eye, that this makes Quaid's glasses flash again. It doesn't come with darkness, but I see it. Her fear of being left behind sparked up his glasses.

"All right," I say, blowing out a breath. "Everyone skootch in."

Aric and Quaid come closer until we're all pressed together, and I close my eyes and manifest a park I saw in the mortal realm.

Nothing happens.

I try again, this time manifesting my home in Olympus.

Nothing happens.

"As I was saying," Quaid sneers. "We've all lost our powers." He looks at Aric. "Well, I don't know what your power is, so maybe you still have it. But something tells me this place is your weakness."

Aric doesn't admit it, but we all know Quaid is right.

He's right about all of it.

Star is the power he needs to get his glasses working again.

Star is the power I need to be able to travel again.

And if the maze is Aric's weakness, then Star must be his strength.

And getting her excited about things is how we get our powers back.

"What the hell are those glasses anyway?" Declan asks.

I hesitate, wondering if I should tell them or not.

Of course, the answer is no. Absolutely not. But there's no way not to. If I don't get a hold of my anger and calm down, they won't help me convince Star to get what I need. Apollo will punish me for giving away his secrets like this, but I'll deal with that later.

So I say, "They're a cheat for the underlying divinity that runs through the fabric of the mortal world. They can rewrite reality. A little bit, anyway. That's how I popped opened the jail cells."

"They can turn walls invisible too," Star says. "We walked through them!"

"That's right," I say. "They seem to work particularly well here in this space. Probably because it's neither Olympus nor the mortal realm. It's something in between. And if we can go through walls, we can get out of here. But only if they're working." I side eye Star. She doesn't like me. Not even a little bit. So she's not gonna like what I'm gonna say next. "I need to... touch her."

"What?" She's appalled. And maybe a little disgusted. "Touch me how?"

I make a face of *come on*, complete with an eye roll, which everyone can see because my sunglasses are no longer dark. But I'm looking at Aric now, not Star.

Aric is the one who has the most control at the moment. I hate that, but it's true. Somehow, he brought us here. Which means, he's got a very big say in how we get out, even if he doesn't realize that yet.

But even though I'm looking at Aric, it's Declan who speaks up next. "You mean... like... sexually?"

I shrug. "It's certainly the fastest way to get her to project some power, but any sustained emotion will do." I look at her now. Straight into those angry eyes. "I could spank you. That would probably do it."

She scoffs. "In your dreams."

Aric actually chuckles. And when I look over at him, he's got a strange smile on his face. In fact, when I glance over at Declan, he's got that same expression.

They're picturing this punishment in their minds.

"Well," Aric says, snapping out of his fantasy of me spanking Star's little bottom. "We'd have to watch. You know, just to make sure it's all on the up and up."

I laugh. "Absolutely."

"Fuck you!" Star says. She was hiding behind Aric for protection just five minutes ago. But she's stepping away from him now. "He's not getting anywhere near me!"

"Star," Declan says, using one of those smooth and easy voices that one reserves for crazy people. "You need to help *us*, help *you*."

I almost guffaw. But I have to hand it to Declan, slimy as that move is, he's charming. He's made himself into the safe one, so to speak.

"Declan! You're supposed to be on my side!" Star is getting excited. And this is just enough emotion for my glasses to flash and turn black. This is real panic on her part. But it doesn't last. In fact, it's gone in an instant.

"Look," Declan says. "Her panic lit up your glasses!"

Star gets a hopeful look on her face. But I

shake my head. "It's not that easy. Panic isn't enough. It's too fleeting. We need to sustain her emotional state for long periods of time. That's how we draw out the power."

Aric chuckles. "Sex. You wanna use sex."

"You're making this up!" Star protests. "This is not a thing. It's not real."

"No?" I ask. And then I cross the space between us, grab her by the waist, and kiss her. My glasses instantly go dark black, the digital display comes to life inside them, and for a moment, everything is outlined in teal green.

She pushes me away and it disappears.

But she knows I'm right now. She knows.

And so does Aric and Declan.

"Wow," Declan says. "That's… amazing."

Aric laughs. "Well, it's… weird. But his glasses did come back to life, Star. It's probably the only way."

I'm sure, if we tried really hard, we could find another way. But why? When this would be the most satisfying?

"No. No way! This is bullshit." But Star knows she's wrong and when neither Aric nor Declan come to her defense, she narrows her eyes at me. Then, she must get a bright idea, because she smiles. "Not with *him*, anyway." I can almost hear her thoughts, that's how obvious she is. Because her eyes dart between Declan and Aric, like she's trying to decide which one she'd rather get spicy with to get us some power. "*He can touch me, but not you!*" She's pointing at Declan.

I shrug. "I like to watch, so whatever."

"You can't watch!" she says. And she's getting a little shrieky now, so the glasses go black again, but like before, it's fleeting. Just a tiny moment.

"If I'm not nearby, how will you power the glasses?" I ask.

Her eyes dart around the room, landing on a dark opening with a beaded curtain as a door. Which is such a teenage décor choice on Aric's part, I nearly snort. "What's in there?" she asks.

"That?" Aric says. "That's a shower. If you wanna take a shower, I'm here for it. Let's go. I volunteer as tribute." Then he slides his leather jacket off, rips his shirt over his head, and starts for the bathroom.

"*Declan*, I said! Not you!" Star's emotional state is exasperation now.

Aric stops and turns. "Fine." Waves a hand at the shower. "Go on then. But I'm gonna stand in the doorway and watch whether you want me to or not. It's not even like you can stop me. The door is made of beads."

I snicker. I guess he's not as stupid as I thought he was because those beads are a feature, not a glitch. "As will I," I say. "That way I get my power and everyone is happy. Right Declan?"

Declan is smiling like an idiot who just won the Powerball. "Uhhh, yeah. Fuck yeah. I'm happy." Then he walks over to Star and takes her by the hand. "Come on little darlin', let's make beautiful, powerful magic together."

13 - STAR

Before I can object, Declan is pulling me towards the bathroom. I look over my shoulder, desperate to find a way out of this humiliating set up, but Declan was my choice, after all, and he seems to be all in as far as the whole "let's get Star excited so we can get our power back" plan.

There's no way I'm asking Quaid for help, that's for sure. And Aric is following behind us like he's about to get the show of a lifetime.

The lights flick on as we enter and then Declan pauses, grinning down at me like he's a teenage boy about to hit a home run with a girl for the very first time. "You ready?"

"*No!*" I say. "I don't even understand what's happening." Then I shoot Aric a look. "And if he's gonna watch, then you're just not allowed to touch me *at all*." I cross my arms here, to make sure they understand that I am very firm on this matter.

"Figures," Quaid mutters.

"You, shut up!" I say, pointing my finger at him. "I'm not talking to you. And you're not allowed to watch, either!"

Declan turns towards the others and beams them a charming smile. "Listen guys, I know you think this is funny, but give her a break. You can't watch, OK? This is serious business. She's got secrets that need to be unlocked and the key to unlocking them is *pleasuring* her." He chuckles those last few words out and then I catch him waggling his eyebrows, like this whole thing is a joke.

"You don't know that!" I protest. "You don't know if any of that is true! This is just some... *fantasy* of yours. And that goes for you too!" I point at Quaid and Aric.

"A fantasy?" Quaid says, sneering at me. "You broke my glasses."

"Which is another fantasy! I didn't do anything!"

"That's enough, you guys," Declan interrupts. He stretches out his arm, putting a barrier between me and the other two. "The whole point of this is to make her feel good."

"Wrong," Quaid says. "The whole point is to work her up. There are many ways to do that."

"I'm gonna go on record here," I say. And I'm looking straight at Declan, not them, when I say this. Because he's the only one who seems to care about what I think. "You're not gonna touch me if they're watching. If you do..." I narrow my eyes. "It will be against my consent.

Quaid huffs out his objection. But to my surprise, Aric gives in. "She's right."

"What?" Quaid can't believe his ears. "You were the one who came up with this idea."

"I know," Aric says, "but... we're not do anything against her will. And while watching Declan wind her up would be fun, I just want out of here. As soon as possible. I don't give a fuck how we get it done. So fine." He turns back to me. "You win. We'll go all the way to the edge of the room. But we're not gonna plug our ears, so I hope for your sake you're not a screamer." Then he shoots me a wink and walks off, leaving Quaid to fight his own battle.

I put my hands on my hips and give my toe a tap. "Well. Are you going to leave, or not?"

Quaid rolls his eyes. "The entire point of this is to power up my sunglasses. How will you do that if I'm not even here?"

"Just move around the corner, at least," I growl.

"It's not gonna work," he says. "You have no idea how it works."

"Neither do you, so let me worry about that."

I say this with a confidence I don't feel, but he does move out of my line of sight, and I guess that's the best I can hope for at the moment.

"Well done," Declan says, slipping his hands around my waist and pulling me towards him and leaning in to kiss me. "Now, let's get started."

I put a stop to that with a very firm hand on his chest. "Are you sure this is the only way?"

"Who cares if it's the only way?" Aric calls from the other room. "It's the quickest way, and that's the only thing that matters."

Declan looks down at me sympathetically. "We know it'll work, Star. Somehow, your emotional state is affecting our powers. How that happened, I don't know. But there's a connection here. You know it's true. And Aric's right. Who cares about the details right now?"

Then Declan lowers his voice to a whisper. "If Aric is afraid of this place, he's got good reasons for it. Does he look like a guy is who is afraid of anything?"

"I'm not afraid!" Aric yells. "I just... don't want to be here."

Declan rolls his eyes, but he's actually very serious. "Think about it, Star. We need to restore our powers and get somewhere safe. Then we can ask the questions. And anyway, it's not gonna be horrible. You and I? We're gonna make out a little, feel each other up, get all acquainted and shit. It was gonna happen anyway, right? I mean… look at me?" I smile, despite my unease and all the strange things that seem to be happening. "Right?" He prods. "If you've got to be wound up by someone, I'm not a bad choice."

It's true, he's not. And I *was* attracted to him. Aric, as well. Maybe not Quaid, but if being wound up by Declan will fix Quaid's glasses, then there will be no reason for Quaid to wind me up afterward.

Yes, Declan is right. There are worse choices than him and he's standing in the other room.

"So that's what we do," Declan continues, taking a step towards me and placing his hand on my cheek. It's both warm and cool at the same time, giving me a little chill. Or, probably more likely, a little thrill. "Then Quaid fixes his glasses and we get out of here. And anyway, we're not gonna take a shower. It's like five minutes of sensual kissing and heavy petting. I'm a good kisser, I promise. You'll see. So… what do you say?" Again, he takes a step towards me. And this is the end of any space between us. His hips are now pressing against me, both hands are on my cheeks, and he's leaning down.

I would like to think I'm not attracted to him. That this whole idea of letting him kiss and touch me to gain enough power to get Quid's shades working again is repulsive. Or at the very least, morally objectionable. But Declan is not just handsome. He's… smooth. Easy. A very different kind of control than I've ever experienced before.

If I have to let one of these men get me sexually aroused, I could do worse than Declan. So I open my mouth to give him permission, but no words come out.

His lips are already pressing against mine, his hands traveling up my body, and then one of them snakes around to grab my ass while the other gently caresses my breast.

It's all very exciting in an unexpected way.

14 - ARIC

"*P*sst," I hiss at Quaid. "Get over here and get to work. They're doing it."

I don't bother waiting for Quaid to answer me because Declan is committed to the mission and he's going for it. He walks Star backwards, still kissing her, until she bumps into the wall.

"Damn, that's kinda hot." Quaid is beside me now.

"Who cares if it's hot," I mutter. "Fix the fucking glasses."

"Wow this place has really gotten you spooked, hasn't it?"

I look over my shoulder at him and growl, "Fix. The fucking. Glasses."

Which makes Quaid chuckle. For a mortal with no power, he's cocky. Which means he's got more going for him than Declan and I understand, but whatever. After I get out of here, I'll never have to see him again.

In the bathroom, having practically pinned her to the wall, Declan is now grinding against Star. But she's not objecting. In fact, her hands start wandering. Reaching around Declan's bare torso. She scrapes her fingernails across his skin, making his back arch. But still, he never stops kissing her.

"How's it coming?" I ask Quaid, unable to take my eyes off the show. It's heating up pretty good. But I would like a progress report.

"Nothing yet."

I turn and look at Quaid. "What?"

He shrugs. "Nothing."

"How could there be nothing? They're practically fucking with their clothes on." As if to illustrate my point, Star begins to moan. And then I catch her hand moving again. This time, it sneaks around to Declan's front and then she grabs his dick right through his jeans.

He pulls out of the kiss for a moment, staring down at Star with hooded eyes. "Fuck yeah, grab it again." But he doesn't wait for her to do this on his own, his large hand cups her tiny one and he begins rubbing himself using her hand to do it.

"Anything?" I whisper to Quaid.

"Nothing."

I force myself to look away from Star and Declan. "What?"

He shrugs. "Nothing. It's doing nothing."

"How is that possible? Just a few minutes ago she was making all sorts of shit happen and she was just angry. Clearly," I pan a hand to the show Star and Declan are putting on, "She's more excited now than she was then. So why isn't it working?"

Quaid is about to answer when four things happen at once.

First, Declan says, "I wanna fuck you so hard right now," making Star moan.

Second, the lights go out and room becomes a darkness so vast, I hold my breath.

Third, in this darkness Quaid's glasses spark and then a sort of electricity shoots out of them.

And fourth, the walls light up with glowing designs. Little symbols, or something. Like an ancient language.

Then three more things happen.

Quaid says, "Stop! You're making it worse! You're glitching my glasses!"

Declan and Star break apart, looking up and around at the glowing walls.

And then the lights come back on.

"What the fuck was that?" I ask.

Everyone is talking at once.

Declan is saying, "Did you see the walls? Did you see the fucking walls?"

And Quaid is saying, "They're fried now! They're fuckin' fried!"

And Star is saying, "I saw you." Except she's not looking at Declan, she's looking at *me*.

A sudden sinking feeling fills my gut. "What?" I ask.

She breaks away from Declan and comes towards me. "I saw you. In here." She points to the ground.

Instantly, I'm transported back in time. A time filled with fear. Nothing but absolute fear. Over the years that fear has faded into embarrassment. It was shameful to me just how afraid I was back then. At just how much this place affected me. How my whole body would quake and shiver every time I woke up from being killed by the monster. And the dread I felt when I realized I'd have to do it all again.

I blink and suddenly, I'm standing in the maze. At a four-way junction. There is one flaming torch lighting up each choice, making the walls flicker eerily as I pause, unable to make a decision and breathing so hard, I think I might pass out.

A hand touches my shoulder and I almost scream like a girl. But when I turn, it's not the monster.

It's Star.

"It's OK," she says. She looks exactly like she does back in my room. Wearing the same clothes and everything—a long black dress with little sparkles on it, making her look like a night-sky princess.

"It's me, Aric. I'm here. You're not alone."

I squint. Whispering, "What?"

"You're not alone."

I blink again and I'm back in the present, the room back to normal. No darkness, no glowing walls.

Quaid's glasses spark and he overreacts, flinging them off his face. They go skittering across the rock floor and end up under the bed. He looks at me "What the fuck was that?"

I shrug. "I have no fucking clue." But then I take my attention to Star. "You were there."

She points at herself, her face still very flushed with the desire she was experiencing with Declan. "Me? Was where?"

"Here." I point to the ground. "I mean, out there." I point to the walls, indicating the maze. "I was back there for a moment, in the maze. I had four choices and I couldn't make up my mind. And then you were there and you said I wasn't alone anymore."

She smiles here. Like... really fucking smiles at me. "Aww. That was nice of me. Did I help you?"

"I blinked and..." I let out a long breath. "Then I was here again."

"What did you see, Star?" This is Declan. "When you saw Aric?"

"Oh, well it was here, but not in the maze. You were..." She doesn't finish. But her eyes glide over to the bed.

"I was what?" I ask. She looks at me with an all-teeth grin, and even though her face is still rosy from being sexually aroused by Declan, they go scarlet now. "What?" I ask. "What did you see?"

She glances at Declan, winces, then shrugs and turns her attention back to me. "You and I were... well, let's just say it was your turn to get me worked up, I guess."

My eyebrows shoot up and suddenly, all the fear is gone. I let out a laugh. "Well, finally something is going my way."

"But did you see the walls?" Declan asks. He's very annoyed at this latest development. "They were all lit up with symbols."

"I did," I say. "I saw them too."

"Well, I didn't," Quaid snarls. "I was too busy being shocked my glasses." Now he glares at Star. "It's you. You're doing this on purpose."

It's Star's turn to laugh. She puts up a hand, palm first, like she's warding him off. "Trust me when I say this, I'm not doing anything to you. Or with you. You're a jerk and I would like you remove this collar from my neck immediately." She looks at Declan. "Please." Begs. "Please make him take it off. I don't like it."

Quaid scoffs. "We already went over this. The

moment it went on, it sealed. There's not even a buckle, Star. You're the property of Apollo now."

Those words hang in the air. Declan and I find each other's gaze and lock eyes. He cocks his head. I cock mine back.

So that's what he up to. I guess I'm not surprised. Looking back, it's obvious.

"What does Apollo want with her?" Declan asks.

"Like he'd tell me," Quaid scoffs.

"I think I understand," I say. Everyone looks at me. "That's why your glasses aren't working. You put that collar on Star and her magic is interfering."

"No fucking shit," Quaid says.

"But it's the collar," I say. "This place belongs to Ares. Apollo has no magic here." I look at Declan. "And neither does Hermes."

"So we're fucked?" Star says.

"No," I say. "Not from what I've seen. Because somehow, your powers have merged with ours."

"How?" Star asks. "I don't have any power."

"You have lots of powers," Declan says. "You're the Eighth Sister of the Pleiades. You *have* to have powers. It's just… a thing with those sisters. I think it's got something to do with the walls and those glowing symbols." He turns to look at me. "Did the walls always glow when you were here?"

I shake my head. "No. That's new."

"See," Declan says. He's smiling now. "I'm right. Her power is in those walls and the symbols written on them."

"So what good is that?" Quaid asks. "Who cares? How do I fix my glasses? Because every time she gets excited, it gets worse, not better."

"I think I know." Everyone turns to look at me. "Think about it. This place is connected to me. When Declan was skipping us out of jail, I was thinking about this place and how I was a prisoner here because obviously, I was a prisoner back there in the jail. My thoughts got mixed up with his transport. Declan and I both brought us here. Then—" I point at Quaid. "Somehow those magic glasses of yours got mixed up with it too when you put the collar on Star."

Star sighs. "That's just great. So I'm stuck with him?"

"We're all stuck with each other," I say. "The four of us? We've been... *merged*."

Ya know, to be honest—I'm not all that upset about being stuck with them. I mean, not Quaid. He can go fuck himself. But Aric and Declan—two gods? Or demigods, maybe? I've never had much interest in ancient history, so the technical jargon isn't exactly second-nature.

But half-god or whole, they're both very hot. Very sexy. And in two completely different ways, which is nice. Declan is all charming and fun while Aric is all stoic and strong.

I don't know what 'being merged' means when it comes to magic, but I can certainly use my imagination for how it might play out in other ways.

A chuckle comes spilling out of my mouth and I blush and look down a little, and when I look up again, for some reason I'm staring at Quaid and he's glaring at me. *Again.* "What?" I snap.

"What are you chuckling about?"

"Nothing."

He turns to Aric. "There's something wrong about her."

"What?" I say.

Aric looks confused. "What are you talking about?"

"Look at her, she's smiling. She's happy. She chuckled. She *did* this."

"I didn't do anything," I say. "That's not why I was smiling, for fuck's sake."

Quaid narrows his eyes at me. "Then why *were* you smiling?"

"It's none of your business."

He laughs. "None of my business? That's funny. You're the whole reason we're here."

"No," I say. Getting defensive. "Aric is. He just said so."

We all look over at Aric who shrugs. "Fuck it, it's my fault, I guess. But like I was saying," and I get a little thrill of satisfaction here, because he takes a moment to scowl at Quaid, "—we've been merged."

"But what does that mean," Declan asks.

Aric takes a moment to think, then shrugs. "I'm no expert on the rules of power distribution in Olympus, but there *are* rules, ya know? And I know how it works under normal conditions."

"How?" Quaid asks. A little too eager, if you ask me.

I think Aric is thinking the same thing, because he throws Quaid a look of suspicion. But he doesn't act on it. "Frequencies," he says.

"Oh, yeah," Declan says. "I knew this. That's how I travel. What's that got to do with anything?"

But I'm looking at Quaid while Declan is talking, and it's pretty clear to me that he *didn't* know this was how power was distributed in Olympus. In fact, he's so intent on listening to Aric's upcoming explanation, he doesn't he noticed me watching him.

Which allows me a few moments to study him. Which, unfortunately, is enough time for me to appreciate that he's... maybe... attractive. In an asshole kind of way.

"Well," Aric says. "Frequencies can be combined. That's not how it works in Olympus, though. So..." He shrugs. "I don't know why it happened here, but I think it did."

"So what's this mean?" Declan asks. And again, Quaid is seriously paying attention to this conversation between the two demigods.

"Well," Aric says, blowing out a breath. "It means that... the rules must not apply to us."

"How do you figure that?" Finally, Quaid asks a question.

"Because," Aric says. "We did it and it shouldn't have happened."

"*He* shouldn't have happened, either," Declan says, pointing to Quaid.

"Yeah," Aric says. "He's an odd one. Let's leave Quaid out of this for a moment and just think about you and me, Declan. We're both demigods who have been given powers by actual gods."

"So have I," Quaid protests. "My power comes from Apollo."

"No," Aric says, looking at Quaid. "You're nothing like us." And the funny thing is, he's not being mean or facetious about it. "I'm not saying you're not important in what's happening. Obviously, you are. I'm just working with what I know for the moment. And what I know is that demigods and gods don't operate under the same power regulations. That's why they make us."

Declan chuckles. "So they can cheat."

Aric points at him. "Yes. Exactly. So they can cheat." Now he looks at me. "Star is a demigod too. Not only that, she was sent to the mortal world to be hidden." His eyes narrow down a little as he stares at me, like he's seeing me for the very first time. And this direct, full attention makes my stomach jump and my heart rate surge. Despite his brutish appearance, there's a lot to like about Aric and I'm very attracted to him. "There's something unique about you, Star."

I really like hearing him say my name and I'm suddenly wondering when Aric and I will take our turn in the bathroom. I can totally picture showering with him.

He smiles at me in this moment, then winks like he's reading my mind.

This makes me blush.

"She's doing it again," Quaid says.

"Doing what?" Declan asks.

"She's got that weird look on her face."

I let out a breath and roll my eyes.

Aric continues. "Something has happened here." He makes a motion with his finger to me, and Declan, and himself. "Something unexpected."

"Something that broke my glasses," Quaid adds. Like he's pissed off that he's not being included in the conversation.

And just to piss him off more, I decide to participate in this conversation even though I have no clue what's going on. We're all standing in a rough circle, Declan on my right, Aric on my left, and Quaid across from me. I reach for Declan's hand, then for Aric's and I tug them closer to me, like they're mine.

Neither of them object. Both of them smile and reach for me, letting go of my hands and slipping their arms around my waist in a similarly possessive move. This causes a thrill of desire and arousal to course through my body and then, something else happens.

The lights go out and there is a brief moment of total darkness. Then… the whole place lights up with those tiny celestial carvings in the walls.

"There!" Declan says, pointing to the walls.

"Yeah," Aric agrees. "I see it. Wow." Then he pulls his arm back from me, like he's unsure, and the glowing stops and darkness fades.

"No!" Declan says, looking at me. "What did you do?"

"It wasn't me," I say, looking up at Aric. "It was him."

"Put your arm back around her," Declan says. "The magic is between us."

"Yeah," Aric agrees. But he doesn't put his arm around me again. "I get that. But… how? And why? What are we doing? This was supposed to be an abduction job and now I'm stuck in the fucking maze and my target is affecting my magic in ways I don't understand."

"Isn't that I good thing?" I ask. Because he's pulling back and I don't want him to.

Declan wraps both his arms around me now, kinda grinding in to me. "More for me, if he's not interested."

And to my surprise, it is Quaid, not Aric, who responds. "I'm interested."

We all look at him. Everyone's eyes

narrowing down in suspicion. "Interested in what?" I ask, unable to hide my hostility.

I get a crooked smile as an answer. "Well, you're the wellspring, Star. And I'd like to take a drink."

Declan chuckles. "Hey, I'm down with sharing."

"No," Aric suddenly says. "*No,*" he says again. "We can't combine the powers."

"Why the hell not?" Declan asks.

"Yeah," Quaid adds. "Why not? They're synergistic, you said it yourself."

"Her and us," he says. "That's the synergy." Then he points to Quaid's glasses, which he's holding in his hand. "*Only* her and us. Because if Declan and I combine, then things get out of hand. That's what broke your glasses, Quaid. It was too much."

"So what's that mean?" I ask. Feeling weirdly disappointed. Because I like them both and I want them both. And now Aric's saying it can't happen.

"I think it means that we each have a synergistic power with you, Star. We make you more powerful and you make us more powerful. But's a duo, not a triad." Then he looks at Quaid. "Or a quad."

"Wow, that's weird," Declan says. "His name is Quaid and with us he makes us a quad."

"My name does not mean four, Declan. It's not weird."

Declan shrugs. "It's still got a Q in it."

Which makes me smile for a moment. But then I look up at Aric and find him frowning. I decide to confront his unease head on. "Why are you so worried?"

Aric lets out a breath. "I'm not worried, exactly. It's just… you're… special."

I smile. "Thank you. I'd like to think so."

But he doesn't smile back. "It's just…" Now he looks around the room. And suddenly I get it. We're in some kind of… trap for him. He was stuck here, fighting the monster, all by himself. And now he's probably worried about how we get out.

So I reach for him, taking his hand as I look up into his eyes. "Don't worry. You're not alone this time."

And finally, he smiles. "You've said that already. But Star, I've got to say, even if you can help me get out of the maze again, I would never ask you to do that. Because you have no idea how bad it's gonna be."

16 - DECLAN

"I think we should start there."

The heavy moment between Aric and Star breaks and everyone turns to look at me.

"Start where?" Quaid asks.

"With them." I point to Aric and Star. "Clearly, they have a strong connection. She saw Aric in the maze and they were already..." I pause here, tying to find the right words. "They were already getting to know each other. And Aric saw her in the maze. Some kind of vision. They were talking to each other. Plus, he knew about her song. He knew the words."

"No," Aric is shaking his head. "She's not gonna run the maze with me."

"Why not?" Star asks.

"*Why not?*" Aric scoffs. "Because we're gonna die, Star. Probably thousands of times. And I don't want you to go through that. It's... soul crushing. I would never ask you to help me. Not at that cost."

Star smiles. "You didn't ask. I offered."

"All of this is pointless," Quaid says. "We can talk about how to get out after we figure out the power structure. Aric, it's not up to you. We're all involved here. If Star wants to use her power to get us out of this maze, then I say yes."

"You would," Aric says. "You're nothing but a selfish piece-of-shit mortal."

"OK," I say, stepping between them. Then I look at Aric. "He's right, though. You're jumping ahead. You and I need to figure out how our powers combine with Star's."

"Figure it out?" Quaid asks. "Figure what out? We've done that part. It's... sexual." And the strangest thing about these words he says, is the way he says them. Especially the last part. Because it comes with a bit of longing.

Which I understand, I guess. He's been left out. He's got no powers to share with Star so, he's jealous. Maybe even feeling a thirst for her, as he hinted a few minutes ago, despite the growing animosity between them.

He's also right. There's no point in pretending. It *is* sexual. I mean, perhaps one could coax our powers into mingling with some exceptional feelings of joy or probably fear, as well.

But sex—it's just too easy compared to that.

Not to mention more pleasurable.

"Go on," I say, pushing Aric towards the bathroom. "It's your turn."

Star looks unabashedly excited about this, so I smile and point to her. "Aric, look at her. She wants you, bro. She *wants* you. Give her what she wants."

"That's not fair," Star says. "I mean, I do want him." Her gaze glides up to Aric's and wow, she really does. It's like she's picturing his cock inside her right now. But then her eyes come back to me and they go a little lazy. Half hooded, so to speak. Like she's got a fantasy of me rolling around in her head as well. "But that doesn't mean I don't want you too."

Funny thing is, it's my cock that gets hard here. Not Aric's. I'm not ashamed to admit I looked. I reach for her, running my fingers through her long, dark hair. "I'll be right here waiting when you're done."

She bites her lip, trying her best not to smile, but not entirely succeeding. And then, inside my head I hear her voice. Her thoughts, actually. *If it were up to me, I'd take you both at once.*

And it's not just a fantasy on my part, because in this same instant, she blushes a very bright pink.

I chuckle. "Any time, darlin'. Just say the word."

"I don't know what you're talking about," Star says.

But she does. And she and I both know that.

There's a connection being made here. Between her and I, and her and Aric and... I like it.

I like all of it.

"Go on," I say, pushing Aric towards the bathroom again. "Quaid and I will hang out over here to give you two kids some privacy."

But it's not me who gets Aric's feet moving, it's Star. She takes him by the hand, encouraging him to follow her with a tug.

Quaid and I glance at each other as they disappear into the bathroom.

He opens his mouth to talk, but I hold a finger. "Bro, you'll get your chance. Don't worry."

"What are you talking about?" he asks. "That's not what I was thinking."

I roll my eyes. "Right. Then what were you thinking?"

"I was thinking... well, wondering actually, if maybe we were all sent here at the same time for a reason."

"Well, sure. We were all sent here to get Star."

"Yeah. We were. But we were assuming that it was for *different* reasons. Or, at the very least, they were separate missions. But what if my god is working with your god—or goddess, as it is— and they're both working with his." He gives a chin nod in the direction of Aric.

"Why would they do that?"

"To see what happens? Because they must know something about Star. Something that makes her desirable. Other than her hot body." Quaid adds this last part with a chuckle.

I point at him. "You like her. You're being a dick, but you like her."

He shrugs. "I'd hit that."

And I laugh. "Yeah, so would I. I mean, there are worse things to be burdened with than a hot little demigoddess who lights up the room with glowing symbols and gets me more power when I work her up."

He frowns. "All she does is break me."

"Maybe," I say, completely understanding his frustration. "I mean, obviously she is interfering with your glasses, that's for sure. But you, Quaid?" I shake my head. "No. She doesn't break *you*."

"You don't get it," he says. "The glasses *are* me. They're the only power I have."

"You're right, I don't get you. I have no idea who you are. But Apollo sent you, Quaid. Which means you're necessary. You should let that be enough for now." Then I slap him on the shoulder. "Come on."

"Where are we going?"

"To watch, of course."

I snicker all the way over to the doorway of the bathroom and then lean up against the wall on one side, while Quaid leans up against the other.

"Shhhhh," I say, putting a finger to my lips.

Then I peak around the corner.

Star and Aric are having one of those awkward sixth-grade, spin-the-bottle moments. In other words, acting like a couple of teenagers who both know they like each other, they're just not sure how to get from first to second base.

Aric mumbles something, which makes Star move in closer to him. Her breasts press up against his chest as her hands move down to his waist and then slowly begin to explore his back. Lucky bastard is already shirtless, having taken it off, so this skin-on-skin contact excites him enough to place his hands on her face and give in. If it was ever a struggle in the first place. Chills erupt all over his tattooed torso and I realize, I'm holding my breath, waiting for them to kiss.

It doesn't disappoint. The moment their lips touch, all the reservations are gone. Aric leans in, opening his mouth, and Star responds by leaning up on her tiptoes. He holds her face in his hands and I'm actually getting excited, heart pounding in my chest, as Star's fingertips play with the button on his jeans.

Next to me, Quaid exhales loudly. "Fuck, that shit is hot."

And I'm about to laugh and agree, when the two lovers just… *disappear.*

17 - STAR

My lips against Aric's feel sensitive and tender, almost charged with electricity. When we first came into the bathroom, there was an awkward moment. Aric was looking down at his feet worried about the maze and how I might be drawn in to it. "I don't want that for you," he whispered. "I wouldn't want anyone to have to run this maze." His gaze came up just enough to look me in the eye. "Honestly, Star, I wouldn't wish that punishment on my worst enemy."

There was so much emotion in that gaze it made my heart skip a beat. So much pent up... anger? Fear? Disappointment?

How must it feel to realize that your own father thought less of you than his worst enemy?

This only drew me further in to this

mysterious man. I pressed up against him, wanting to be closer. My nipples peaked in anticipation as they pushed into his chest and my hands started wandering across his hips, fingertips dragging along the bare skin of his back.

I knew the kiss was coming, even before Aric leaned down. So I rose up on my tiptoes to meet him halfway. When our lips touched—my god, it sent a shock through my whole body. And then the kissing, which started slow and filled with hopeful expectations turned into something more like lust.

That's when the shift happened.

Aric and I both pull apart at the same time. I gasp, and in the same moment, he says, "Oh, fuck. What did we do?"

It's dark where we are, so I don't know what's happening other than, we are no longer in his bathroom. "Where—"

Suddenly, Aric is behind me, one hand clasped tightly over my mouth, the other snaked possessively around my waist, holding me close to him. "Shh," he whispers in my ear. "Don't say anything."

I have a million questions, but Aric does not loosen his hand over my mouth, so I can't ask them. He's looking around, almost frantically.

And then I hear what he's looking for. A

snort, off in the distance. And then I smell it. The stench of *animal.*

Aric begins to back up, looking around as he goes. We take about ten steps like this and then he pulls me off the main corridor and into a side path. "No talking," he whispers, still pulling me backwards with him. "Don't say anything until I get us somewhere safe." We round a corner, then he takes his hand off my mouth, spins me forward as he turns, takes my hand, and starts to *run.*

As if this couldn't get any weirder, something else happens. The walls begin to sing. A note here, a melody there. And words too. I can't make sense of them, but I can clearly hear a *song*!

My song.

And even though he's a big guy, he's not slow. So much faster than me, I'm being pulled along. And the faster we go, the quicker the song becomes. The beat of the music matches the panicked rhythm of my heart.

We go around down a hallway, take a right, then a quick left, then down another hallway, take a left and a quick right, and then, even though I'm nearly ready to fall over, breathless from the hard run, he kicks it up a notch and starts running faster.

At this point, he's literally dragging me and there's no way for me to go on. So I just stop. Which almost lands me face first on the ground, because he doesn't. And if he didn't let go of my hand, I probably would've face planted. "Stop," I say, trying to keep my voice low, but having a hard time because of my ragged breathing. "Stop! I can't go any further."

He doesn't even respond, just swoops me up in his arms and before I can even blink, we're on the move again.

At this point, I'm fuckin' terrified and I'm just about to start throwing a fit, and force him to stop and explain what the hell is happening, when we come upon a door. He opens it, we go inside, and then he sets me down, slams the door closed, and leans against it.

Those eyes of his, when his gaze meets mine, are filled with terror. "Are you OK?" He asks. And he's not even out of breath.

Even though I didn't run that last hundred-yard dash, I am still finding it very difficult to breathe. "What," I wheeze, "is going on?"

"Don't worry," Aric says. "We're safe here."

And that's when I realize, I know where we are. We're in his room. The very one we left when we started kissing. Only there's no sign of Declan and Quaid.

"The kiss," Aric says. "The kissing. Don't you get it? You took out of the present and sent us into the past!"

"What?" I scoff. "That's impossible!"

"Look around, Star. This is my room. We

were just there." He points to the bathroom, which is dark. But the same beaded curtain is hanging in the doorway. "This isn't the present. Look!" He points to the bed, which was made up perfectly when left, but is now a mess of covers and pillows. "And look there!" He points to the place where the holographic strippers in cages were, but aren't now. "This is the past, Star. This is a moment from my fucking past! I haven't beaten the maze! I haven't killed the Minotaur! We're back!"

I look around, nearly in a blind panic. But when I turn back to Aric and see the fear in his eyes—I... I become... *strong*. I think. I feel a sudden protectiveness over him. And an anger. At his father, the god Ares, for putting this man through hell as a child. At all of this. And the unfairness of it.

I walk over to him, slip my arms around his waist, and press my head into his chest. "It's OK," I say. "This might look like the past, Aric, but it's not. I wasn't there and I'm here now." I look up at him, find him looking down at me with such... vulnerability, I nearly come undone. "I'm here now," I say again. "And you're never gonna run this maze alone again. Not ever."

There's a moment where he doesn't say anything. Doesn't move, not one inch. But then he lets out a scoff. "Little Star, the Eighth is gonna save me, huh?"

I nod, pressing my lips together to hide my smile before saying, "That's right. Little Star the Eighth is gonna save you."

His breath comes out of him in a long, slow exhale. Then he takes a quick one in, and he's talking. "The music saved me. I didn't know what it was back then. I only knew that if I ran, the walls would sing. The faster I went, the more words I got. They never made any sense, not at first. It was just jumbled music. Like I was underwater."

"I heard it," I say, excitement in my voice. "I heard it! I think it was my song!"

"*Our* song," Aric corrects me. "It was you, I think. Singing to me all those years ago. Urging me to try harder. To keep going. You're the reason I got out. I followed your voice and it led me to a control room."

I back up a little so I can look up at him. "A control room?"

"Yeah. Like... the maze was a game. And someone was controlling it. My father, obviously. I always knew it had to be somewhat fake because I was the only one in here. And in the real Labyrinth, there were always people in there trying to beat the Minotaur and find the secret cache of treasure."

"It was like a training ground," I say.

"Well, I hadn't thought of it that way, but...

maybe. It doesn't matter anymore because your brother..." He stops here.

"My brother?"

"Theseus. He killed the Minotaur. About a decade back. And you know what the most ironic thing is? There was no treasure. Well, it was metaphorical, I guess. The treasure was freedom from anyone ever having to run the Labyrinth again."

"And my brother did that?"

Aric nods. Then lets out a long breath. "But I guess that's not the end of the story, is it? Because if it was, what the hell are we doing here? And more importantly, how the fuck do we get out? Because if it was the song that got me out, and you were the one singing the song—" He scoffs. "Well, you're here now. Inside the maze. And you've got no idea what I'm talking about."

He's got a point, but I suddenly feel too tired to think about it. And since we're in a safe place, I allow myself this weariness. I take his hand and start walking over to the messy bed.

He follows, but with a bit of reluctance. "What are you doing?"

"Let's just..." I let out a long breath. "Rest. Just for a minute. That run did me in. I don't know how you go so fast. You must have a distant relation to Declan."

This makes him scoff, but it's a good-natured

one. And he lets me win. Because when I get in the bed and lie down, he does the same.

I turn on my side so I can see him. "I liked you from the beginning, you know. I really did."

"That's because I put a curse on you." He points down to his belt buckle. "With this. The reason you fell for me was because of the magic in the belt buckle. Ares gave it to me to make sure I brought you back."

I lean up on my elbow, curious about this. "What does he want with me?"

Aric scoffs again, only this time there's no lightness in it. "Like he would tell me. I might be his son, but in his eyes, I'm just a bastard to be used in his game with the other Olympians."

"And the Titans too," I add. "Because that's what Quaid said. That some cult is after me."

"Yeah," he sighs. "I'd forgotten about that."

I lie back down, but this time, I snuggle up to him. "Thanks for getting me out of danger in the maze."

Which makes him smile. "Thanks for showing me the way out."

"It probably wasn't me, ya know. You're the one who knew the song and the lyrics. I just had a melody that came out of a dream."

He turns his head to look at me, smiling. Then he reaches for a piece of hair that had fallen over my face, and smooths it back, out of my eyes. "You're the dream, Star. In my eyes, anyway. And for the record, I liked you too. Even though it was the magic that made you like me back."

I sit up a little then climb on top of him. Straddling his hips and pressing my hands on either side of his head. My long, dark hair falls over my shoulders like a waterfall, brushing against his cheeks. "It wasn't the magic."

And then, without even asking, I lean down and tenderly place my lips on his.

The spark of passion is immediate, but when he kisses me back, I feel like a fire ignites inside me. His hands grip my hips, as he arches his back a little, lifting me up. A tease for what could come next—if I want it.

And I do.

Reluctantly, I pull back from the kiss and scoot backwards a little, just enough to give me access to his belt. A moment later, my fingers have released the buckle and I'm tugging on the button of his jeans. This whole time, our eyes are locked. All I see is him and all he sees is me.

Suddenly, he flips me over onto my back, pulls his zipper down, reaches inside his pants, and pulls out his cock. He strokes himself a few times, hovering over me like a promise.

Then he reaches for the neckline of my dress and pulls it down. The elastic gives, allowing him to expose my bra. Then he pulls that down too, and immediately, my nipples rise up into hard peeks. Aric's lips lower down over one, then he's sucking on me.

My fingers find their way into his dark hair, gripping his head to encourage him. He nips me, making me hiss, but at the same time, his hand has found its way between my legs. In one swift motion, he's pulled my panties aside and his finger begins stroking my sweet spot and pushing up inside me.

The wetness spills out, letting him know I'm ready for whatever he wants to do next. His finger probes deeper, setting me off and making my back arch. I feel his hard cock pressing against my inner thigh and all I want is for him to be inside me now.

"I'm ready," I whisper. "I want your cock."

But he just grins at me with a mischievous gleam in his eyes. "Oh, I bet you do, Miss Star. But I've got more in store for you than just mere cock."

He sucks on my breast again, squeezing them with just enough force to drive me wild. Then he takes his kisses down my stomach. I hold my breath and begin to writhe, urging him on. To make his mouth reach his final destination between my legs in haste. But he chastises me by pinching a nipple hard enough to make me squeal.

"Patience, bright one. I'll get there when I'm good and ready."

I bite my lip as his mouth reaches the triangle of soft hair between my legs. But I let out a loud moan when he backs up and using firm hands on the inside of my knees, opens up my legs, fully exposing my glistening pussy.

Our eyes meet, mine barely open, I'm so turned on. And he grins, licking his lips, before lowering his head down. His fingers move up my inner thighs, parting the lips of my pussy, and the first stroke of his tongue sends me into a fit of frenzied wriggling.

Then his whole mouth is on me, sucking and licking me. Hitting that sweet spot over and over again until I'm on the verge of climax.

That's when he pulls back, sitting upright with his legs parted and his long, thick cock sticking straight up between them.

I whimper, "No! Don't stop."

But he just smiles in response as he strokes himself. "Watch me," he says. His voice a low growl. "Watch me jerk off, Star. I want you to look at it."

I do, without hesitation. His big hand wrapped around his solid dick. He makes a full stroke. His hand coming up and over the tip each time and then going all the way back down to the base.

Then he grabs my hand and places it over his. My small, teeny, tiny hand over his makes him moan and begin to thrust his hips. Getting in to the motion.

"Don't come," I say. It comes out like a beg. "I want you to be inside me when you do that."

"Oh, don't worry," he chuckles. "I'm not even close to coming. I like a long tease, my little brilliant bit of light. I want you to fuck me with your hand until I can't stand it anymore."

He removes his hand, leaving mine in place. I grip him hard, making him moan as he throws his head back. I pump him faster. Grip him tighter. And the wetness between my legs becomes a pool of longing.

"Yes," he saying. Moving his hips with the rhythm of my hand. "Yes. Jerk me, Star. Get me good and ready so I can explode inside you—"

That's it, I can't take it anymore. I want him and I want him now!

Holding tight to his cock, I lift my hips up and press the tip against my wet pussy. "Now," I say. "And don't tell me no. I want it now."

He gives in, thrusting inside me, making my back buckle from the force and pressure. It's painful at first, but in a blissful way. And it fades quickly, far too quick for my preferences.

Then we are fucking. Real, feral fucking. His hips are pounding into mine, his cock pushing deep, deep inside me. Sliding against the walls of my pussy with the perfect amount of friction.

I grab his hair, pulling his face down to me,

and when he kisses me, that's it—I'm so completely fulfilled, I let the release come without a single bit of hesitation.

He groans, biting my lip, and then I feel his climax too. His hot seed spilling inside me as we writhe on the bed like animals.

My eyes are closed, but a light shines its way past my lids, making me open them as the pleasure continues to course through my body.

I gasp, looking up at the ceiling. "Oh, my god! What is that?"

Aric turns, looking up as well, and then he laughs at the glowing symbols covering the stone walls of the room. That's when the music starts. The melody that's been a nagging earworm since I was a child.

Only it's no longer a melody, it's an orchestra of harmony. Like the notes I was hearing was just a fragment of what could be.

And what could be is… Aric and me.

The next thing I know, the glowing symbols are gone and the light in the room changes.

"What the fuck?"

Aric and I both gasp as the voice, because it's Declan. And he's across the room, in front of the beaded curtain of the bathroom, staring at us in the bed. All hot, and sweaty, and satiated from the sex.

18 - QUAID

I'm still staring at the empty bathroom when Declan turns and says, "What the fuck?"

I turn as well, unable to believe my eyes. Because Aric and Star are in the bed across the room. Aric is on top of her and Star's dress and bra have been pulled down, revealing her tight nipples and firm breasts.

"Holy hell," Declan moans. "You two look fuckin' hot. Did you just have sex?" He looks over his shoulder to the bathroom. Then back at our new couple in the bed. "But... you were..." He hikes a thumb behind him. "Over there. Just one second ago. Aric's dick wasn't hanging out of his pants and Stars tits weren't spilling out of her dress so what the hell just happened?"

It's a good question. And I'd be thinking the

same thing… if I wasn't too busy staring at Star's tits and flushed face. I don't know why this girl turns me on—especially when she's in bed another man after having sex with him.

But she does.

My dick wants to get hard *so bad*.

But I force myself to control it. She shouldn't have that kind of power over me. It's dangerous.

Aric gets up out of bed and starts using a t-shirt on the floor to clean himself up. His cock is *huge*. Not that I'm looking, but my god.

Star is so tiny. I bet she moaned when he packed that monster inside her. Loud. Maybe even squealed.

I'm not a small guy and my cock is quite the specimen. Probably pretty equal to Aric's. Which means she'll probably squeal and moan like that when I'm inside her too.

If I ever get that chance.

Star is struggling to put her tits back inside her dress, but she's having some trouble with the bra and getting flustered, which never helps. So Declan and I get a nice long look at her breasts as Aric comes to the rescue and helps her get everything sorted.

Declan scoffs. "Well, don't put her back together too quickly there, Aric. She's not done yet."

God, he's so… blunt. He's got no tact at all. But he doesn't even seem to realize it and no one seems to care. But I guess if I was a demigod, I wouldn't give a fuck what other people thought about me either.

"Why don't we just concentrate on what they learned," I say, side-eyeing Declan. "Instead of how you want Star in a perpetual state of sex-readiness."

"Sex-readiness," Declan laughs. Then looks at Star. "Would you hate it if I kept you naked in bed all day, Star? Ready for one of us to rock your world?"

I except a pretty big protest over this remark, but Star actually *smiles* at him. She doesn't like... agree or reply yes or no, either way, but it sure seems to me like she's taking this offer seriously.

Fuckin' demigods. They can get away with anything.

Aric is back in the bed now, cleaning Star up between her legs—so he's blocking our view. Which is kind of an unexpected behavior, coming from him. In my opinion, at least. He's been projecting a very brutish demeanor this whole time we've been together. But he's different with her.

It's confusing.

Declan elbows me. "You wanna go next?"

I scoff and look at him. "What?"

"I think you should go next. Your glasses are a pretty important piece of this puzzle. I'm just the ride out of here."

I look over at Star to see if she heard him, and I think she did because Aric has finished his task and she's looking right at us. But she doesn't say anything.

"What do you think, Aric?" Declan says. "Should Quaid go next?"

Aric's dick, despite having been cleaned up, is still hanging out of his pants. "Bro," I say. "Put that thing away already."

He tugs on it, then winces. "It won't fit back in my pants until it calms down a little. So don't look at it if you don't wanna see it."

Which makes Declan guffaw and Star go bright red.

And me... I just... *hate him*. For being so... himself. And he wasn't even being an asshole when he said that, his giant cock not fitting back into his tight jeans after sex is just an annoying detail that he's learned to live with.

What must his life be like? Both of them, actually. The privilege and opulence they live in, not to mention a direct lineage to the gods, must be what gives them this sense of confidence and superiority.

It's something you're born with.

Because it's certainly not something I've ever felt.

Something I will never know.

And I'm not saying I want to be someone other than me, it's just... the distance between the life I lead and theirs—it's literally another world.

We are not the same.

Declan claps me on the back. "All right, since you've got no objection, you're up friend. Go get her."

I shrug his hand off me, and shoot him a look. "Maybe we should ask Star what she wants?"

"What she wants?" Declan laughs. "She wants us, Quaid. Look at her. She's all hot and sweaty. Her cheeks are all pink from Aric making her come so hard. What she wants is *more*."

"Give it a rest," I say. Because apparently no one else is gonna stop him. Not even Star.

She's looking at me now. Our eyes are locked. But she doesn't object. Not to Declan's outburst or the idea that I'm next.

Aric walks over to us, his dick having finally shrunk enough for him to begin stowing it away, and he just nonchalantly says, "All right, Declan, that's enough. Let's give these two kids some privacy. Quaid here seems to have sex hang ups. He's not like us and doesn't want an audience." Declan is immediately protesting, but Aric just grabs his arm and pulls him over to the door where we initially came in. "We're gonna check out the maze, Quaid. Be back in a few."

And that's what they do. They fuckin' leave.

So... yeah. There's no one here but Star and me.

She composes herself first, sitting up in the bed so she can give the pillows a good plump. "You might as well just go with it, Quaid."

Which is typical, I guess. She's one of 'them'. A demigod with power, and secrets, and prophecies swirling around her like a little whirlwind in the desert. Oblivious to her special status and what makes us so different.

I don't move. I'm just not sure what I'm doing here.

"Come on," she says. Patting the bed next to her. "Take off your coat and shirt and just... try."

"Try?" I scoff. "I don't need to try anything. I'm not hesitating because I'm nervous, Star."

"Then what is it?"

"You don't like me. And this is just a job. I'm not..." But I falter here.

"You're not what?" And the funny thing is, she's not hostile, even though I'm definitely being belligerent with her. Her voice is soft and even.

"I'm not like them," I say. "I'm not... one of them. I'm not one of *you*."

"So you're afraid that you're gonna underperform?"

"Fuck's sake, is promiscuous sex a trait with you fuckin' demigods, or what? No, I'm not afraid of underperforming. I'm pretty confident my dick will satisfy you. I'm just a traditional guy. I'm… selective. I don't pleasure myself with just anyone, OK?"

"So I'm not good enough for you?" Again, her rebuttal is not heated. Not meant as a challenge. She pats the bed again. "Come on. Tell me more. You can even keep your clothes on." She points to herself. "Look, I've got mine on."

Which is true, she's fully dressed.

But just minutes ago, her tits were hanging out and Aric's semen was all over her inner thighs.

"You're not jealous, are you?"

I don't say anything.

"Oh, my god, you are. Why? You don't even like me. We're supposed to have sex, or whatever, so we can get out of here."

"And that's OK with you?" I ask.

"Yes. But…" She hesitates.

"But? But what?"

"Well… I don't know how long this is gonna last, but regardless, at this point in time, we're all connected. And you're definitely part of that connection, Quaid. And despite our initial hostility, I'm OK with the plan."

"The plan. To use me for my glasses."

"Wow. You have baggage."

"Well, it's true, isn't it?"

She lets out a breath. "Am I pretty?"

"What?" I'm scoffing again.

"Am I pretty?"

"Do you need me to confirm that for you? Are you looking for me to pump up your ego? Because I'm pretty sure Declan does that enough for all three of us."

"No. I'm asking if I'm your type, Quaid. Like… maybe you prefer blondes? Or taller chicks? I'm pretty short. Or perhaps my personality just doesn't do it for you. That's what I'm asking. Because if that's the case, we can keep it professional. I won't get attached. I'll let you work me up just enough to get what we need, and then I'll pull back. But if it's not, Quaid, and we're gonna be stuck together for the foreseeable future, then I'd like to mend the fence between us and allow it to go where it goes."

Go where it goes? I squint my eyes at her. "Are you… picturing some kind of relationship between the four of us outside of this situation? Because, I'm not gonna be a part of that."

"Why not? Because I'm not your type?"

"Well, first of all, I'm not a demigod. And you're going back to Olympus with both of them," I say, hiking my thumb to the door behind me. "Or one of them, at least. And I'm mortal. So…"

"Oh, I see. I guess I hadn't thought of that."

Which makes sense. She didn't even know who she was when we found her. She still doesn't know who she is, not really. Which means I'm maybe... possibly... being... unreasonable here.

"But what if you could come?"

"To Olympus." I shake my head. "It's not possible."

"Why not? If they can cross to this realm, why can't you cross over there?"

"I dunno. It's just the rules."

"If it's just the rules, then someone made those rules. Which means the rules can change."

"Anyway," I sigh. Because this is a nowhere conversation if ever there was one. "What about the collar? You were pretty pissed off about that."

"We'll figure it out."

"Yeah, we will, I guess. When I take you back to Apollo."

"Are you going to take me back to Apollo?"

It's an honest question. One I can't really answer. Partly because if it comes down to me against Declan and Aric, I'm pretty sure one of them will come out on top way before I do. And partly because if I had a choice, no. I would keep her. If she was my type. And she might not be. "You could be my type," I say. Trying to close the distance between us. "You are pretty."

She smiles. And it's a real, honest smile. "OK. Now we're making progress."

"You don't care?" I ask. "That we're all here to use you, Star?"

"I do, it's just… I don't think it's going that way, Quaid. It was at first, but after being with Aric…" She shrugs.

"You like him."

She nods. "I do. And he likes me too, I think."

"So you want to be with him?"

"Well, he's part of *us*. And I'm OK with it. Are you OK with it?"

"With you being with him?"

"Yes." She winks at me. "I've heard that you're one of those traditional guys. Suits, and ties, and monogamy."

"What's wrong with that?"

"Nothing. But there's more than one way to be monogamous."

I actually laugh. It's not a hostile one, either. It's just amusement. "You want all of us."

"Why wouldn't I?" She laughs too. "I mean, look at you, Quaid. I can't see much with all those clothes on, but I'm pretty sure if you took that shirt off, you'd have abs I'd want to lick. And Aric's cock is…" She sighs. "God, the things I could do with that cock."

"What about Declan?" And to my surprise, again, my question is not heated. I'm just… intrigued. Because I've never heard of a woman who wanted three men all to herself. It's fucking crazy. Especially when two of them are demigods.

"Oh, he just looks fun," she giggles.

"What about me? I mean, besides the abs?"

"Well, you're the serious one. Kind of opposite to Declan. But it works for you. Are you one of those considerate lovers, Quaid? Who likes to please?"

My guffaw is so loud, it actually startles her.

"What's so funny?" she asks.

"*No*, Star. *NO*. I am not a considerate lover. I'm not picky about my women because I'm looking for a *wife*. I'm picky because I'm looking for a submissive. And I like to keep it neat, that's all."

"Oh. My god." She puts her hand over her mouth and just blinks at me for a few moments. "You're serious."

"I'm dead fuckin' serious."

"Well. I totally had you all wrong. Why didn't you just say so?"

"Say what? I like to spank and choke? And sometimes I can't control it so I need to be very careful with the women I choose to sleep with? Trust me, that's not how it's done. In this day and age... well," I let out a long breath. "I'm sure you understand."

She studies me, probably running that one sentence over and over in her head. *And sometimes I can't control it...* "So we need a safe word."

"What?" I laugh again. "What do you know about safe words?"

"Believe it or not, I'm actually pretty traditional too. I'm picky about men. I don't have one-night stands. I'm loyal, I guess. But I read a lot. Romance. Most of it the spicy variety. So I'm versed in what you're talking about."

I'm shaking my head. "If you think what you read in books describes what I'd want to do to you, you're wrong."

"What would you do to me? Spank and choke, obviously. But what else?"

"Control you, of course. Every part of your life."

"So sharing would kind of put a damper on that?"

"Well, it would definitely be different. A different type of control, I mean."

"You would want to control me when I was with them?"

I was getting to this, but it hadn't fully manifested in my thoughts yet. "I could see it going that way, I guess."

"Sounds fun."

My eyebrows go up. "You're joking."

"I'm serious."

"What would they think?" I nod my head towards the door.

Star shrugs. "I don't think they'd agree every time we're together, but they'd play along. Declan would definitely play along."

She's right. Declan would play along. He's very easy going.

"He might even let you control him too," Star adds. "Every once in a while."

Which puts an intriguing spin on things. Controlling a couple? Now that's not something you get a chance to do every day. "I hadn't considered that," I admit.

"Well, you should. But before we can get to the specifics of our future relationship—" she pats the bed again. "We need to figure out our present one."

It's gonna happen. I know it now. I'm gonna fuck her, and we're gonna figure out the next step, that's a given. But the future, as enthralling as it might be, is still the future. So she's right. We need to stay in the present. "Your safe word is Aric."

"Aric?" she laughs.

"Because I'll know that you're asking him to come save you."

She nods. "OK. Aric is my safety net."

I reach up and begin unknotting my tie. Star is watching me with a smile, but doesn't say anything. I throw the tie on the bed and point to it. "Don't touch it."

She giggles a little. "Yes, sir."

I shake my head at her.

"Too soon?" she asks.

"Much too soon."

"Sorry."

"It's OK. You'll learn." I take off my suit coat and begin unbuttoning my shirt. Her eyes track my fingers all the way down to my stomach. As I'm taking the shirt off, her eyes dart to my cock. "Up here," I say, my voice stern.

She looks up at me. "What?"

"Eyes," I say. "They stay on mine one-hundred percent of the time."

"If you don't like 'Yes, sir' then how should I respond to that command?"

"You don't. You simply do what I tell you. There's a lot to learn here, Star. So for now, just keep quiet as much as possible."

She presses her lips together, nodding.

Which pleases me. Some women will actually say something back to this. Which is stupid since I just basically told them to shut up. When they do this, it almost never works out. So Star has promise. She has a dominant side to her, for sure. She didn't wilt under my pressure earlier. She snapped back. I like that too, just not during sex. During sex, the only sounds I want to hear are moaning and squealing. Sometimes, I let them beg for things. But it's a reward that needs to be earned.

The shirt now off, I unbuckle my belt. I wait for Star to slip up and look down at my hands, but she doesn't. Her eyes stay locked on mine. Even when I pop the button on the pants and pull the zipper down, she's committed to my command.

But she does break when I pull the cock out. It's already hard. Her submission did that. And she can't help herself. Her eyes dart down and I catch her licking her lips as she gets her fist look at what I have to offer.

I should punish this mistake, but I don't. Because lip licking is cute, and she's new at this, and… well, I just want to get to the good stuff.

But her mistake is noted and I fully plan on testing her on this in the future.

If we do actually have one, that is.

She looks back up at me, wincing. But she doesn't apologize, which earns her a few points.

I step out of my pants and stand in front of her fully naked now. Then I point to the floor in front of me. "Get up and stand here. I'm going to take off your dress."

She sucks in a breath, but it's not nervousness. It's anticipation.

Which is thrilling. Because it's been a long time since I had such a willing partner.

She gets up, standing before me, and never once did her gaze stray from mine. I reach down, grab my cock, and jerk it a little. It's a bit of a test, but mostly I do it for my own benefit.

I really want to fuck her now.

But I need to get this dress off, so I concentrate on that by putting my hands on her shoulders and turning her around so I can access the zipper.

She stands still, but her skin prickles up with goosebumps when I purposefully let my fingers brush against her spine as I drag the zipper down to the small of her back. When I reach in and slide my hands around to her breasts, I can feel her hard nipples even through her bra.

I lean in to her neck, my lips right against her ear, and say, "You're doing so good. You're a very good girl."

She sucks in a breath, but stays quiet as I slip her dress over her shoulders and let it drop to the floor in a puddle at her feet. Then I reach between her legs, find her panties wet with the remnants of Aric's semen and her own juices, and am surprised to realize that it doesn't spur on an episode of jealousy. I'm usually a dick when it comes to that shit. I've never shared a woman.

But Aric... I don't know. I don't see him as competition. I don't think he sees me that way, either. I did make him her safe word, after all. An interesting development that I will need to think on later, but all that can be sorted in the future. Right now, we just need to figure out how I fit into her little magic system.

I hook my fingers into her panties and drag them over her hips and thighs until they too, drop to the floor at her feet.

Next, I unhook her bra, letting it hang on her arms at her elbows as I fondler her breasts for a few moments. When I'm satisfied with that, I step around to her front, push her arms together, and let the bra join the dress and the panties.

Then I just look at her. For being so small, she's got nice wide hips. Almost an hourglass figure. Her breasts aren't overly big, but they are very perky and tight. She blushes at my full attention, which is why I do it. I like them to blush. It's kind of a challenge back at me, if they don't. A red flag that we'll have trouble in the future.

But Star is sending me all the right signals. And if someone had asked me back in that jail cell if I could see her as my next sub, I'd have laughed out loud.

Yet, here we are.

I reach over and play with her long, dark hair as I lock eyes with her again. "You're perfect."

She smiles in response. Clearly delighted to please me.

Which makes me want to please her.

Normally, I'd probably start choking her now. But I'm not sure that's the way to get what we need. Which is answers. So instead, I point to the bed. "Lie down on your back."

She does this by slowly lowering her hands onto the bed and crawling in. Giving me the perfect back view of her glistening pink pussy.

Then, it's gone. Because she turns over, completing my command.

I crawl onto the bed, place my hands on her knees to open her legs, and slide between them. Then I grab her hips and pull her close to me so that the shaft of my dick is pressing up against her wet and open pussy.

She's biting her lip now, clearly ready, and I'm not interested in teasing her any further. So in one well-practiced movement, I reach up with my hand, press it against her throat, and at the same time, the other hand expertly positions my cock at her entrance.

A moment later, I press and thrust. Slipping inside her as my hand starts the choke.

Her eyelids flutter and I wait for it.

I wait for her to see the stars....

19 - STAR

The pressure on my neck is both exciting and scary. I've never done anything like this before, and if I were ever going to start a new life in the world of doms and subs, I would one-hundred percent not choose a guy like Quaid.

I would choose someone less intense. Someone more comfortable showing emotion. Someone who wanted to explore the softer side of control. Because Quaid doesn't seem to have a soft side.

Which should frighten me—but it doesn't.

Perhaps I am naïve?

More likely, I am just stupid.

Because he's a very serious person and even though our conversation beforehand felt in depth while we were having it, I find that the pressure of his hand on my neck is much more of a turn on than I expected.

It's dangerous. I understand this on a rational level, but... it feels good. And in this moment, when the darkness is encroaching on my vision like a hood being thrown over my head, all I can feel is anticipation.

"Stars," he whispers. "See the stars."

At first I think he's calling me by name, but then the stars appear and I know he's not. I understand where this is going and it's... beautiful. The tiny bits of light start as pinpricks. The space around them more gray than black.

But it only takes a moment for that to change. For the lights to brighten and expand while the black turns to emptiness.

I am lightheaded, gasping for air, and then... the song is all around me and I'm running through a maze. I don't stop and listen, of course—one doesn't stop in the middle of your flight-or-flight response to ponder the specifics of the situation— but I fully understand that the Minotaur is behind me and I am running for my life.

Two seconds ago I was in bed, being sexually choked out by a man who absolutely knows what he's doing, and ready to have the orgasm of my lifetime—and now I'm in this damn maze being chased by a monster.

"Faster!" Quaid yells behind me. "Go faster!"

I glance behind me, find his panicked face urging me on, and kick it up into my last gear. We're wearing clothes in this dream—or whatever it is—but just barely. I'm wearing my dress, but no bra, and my flopping girls are not happy about the running. I have no shoes—which seems to be OK since the floor is very smooth stone.

Quaid is also half-dressed. Like we were interrupted while getting dressed. He's got no shirt or shoes, just pants.

"Faster," he says again. "It's gaining on us!"

I try, I do. But I don't have another gear and I'm just about to panic when Quaid passes me—grabbing on to my hand as he goes by—and begins pulling me down the corridor.

"We're almost there!" he yells. "Sing it!" And when I look up ahead of us, he's pointing at something. Bright lights glowing on the dark stone walls.

Symbols. Like the ones we've seen a few times. But I seem to be missing some critical information, because even though I understand that 'sing it' is most likely referring to my earworm, this isn't my song. It's Aric's and I've only heard it once while I was in the middle of a very stressful situation just like this one. And at no point in time did anyone explain to me that there would be a pop quiz on that fucker, so why the hell would I memorize the words?

But to my surprise, I do know the words. And they come spilling out of my mouth. It's not in tune, in fact, its kind of shrieky, but nonetheless, singing it badly seems to be enough. Because as soon as I finish with 'A final gift to be your eyes', Quaid's glasses flash a bright light and everything becomes... I don't know. Dreamy. Foggy. Spinny.

I don't think spinny is a word, but it does describe what's happening because suddenly Quaid and I are slowly *rotating up in the air!*

He's reaching for the lights on the stone wall, while I'm focused on the charging Minotaur that just came around the bend.

The first thing that hits me is the smell. It's monstrous. But then, all I see are teeth.

My heart aches for a second, picturing Aric running from this thing for five years. But there's literally no time to wax poetic about that, because he's covering ground like a damn racehorse in the Kentucky Derby!

"Hurry!" I scream. "Hurry up!"

These words come out of my mouth, but I don't know why. Or what Quaid is doing behind me. All I know is that he's interacting with the lights on the wall.

"I've got it," he says. "Last one and—"

I blink. Blink again, because the light I so

bright, I have to put a hand up over my eyes.

"What the hell did you just do, Star?"

I look to my right and find Quaid standing next to me. He's naked. I look down at myself, find me in the same state, and then look out at the horizon. We're on some kind of a cliff overlooking a peaceful summertime valley.

I look back at Quaid. "I didn't do this."

"Well, it wasn't me. I don't normally interrupt my fucking and choking to go into a dream."

"Hmm." That's all I say back. Because yeah, when you're on the verge of having the best orgasm of your life, you don't generally want to interrupt that with a paranormal experience. But then the maze comes back to me and I turn to him. "Oh, my god, were you there? In the maze with me? Did you see it?"

"What are you talking about?"

"The maze! The Minotaur! It was chasing us and we were running towards a wall with glowing symbols. I had to sing the song, and we floated up into the air, and you were fucking with the lights, and then..." I blink. "Well, a big flash of light occurred and we came here."

He's shaking his head. "Nope. That's not what I saw."

"What did you see?"

"Code. Like... I was inside a computer, or something."

"Like the green outlines in the maze?"

"No, it was literally code. All around me. Like those symbols on the walls that you light up." We stare at each other for a moment. Then he says, "That's your power. That's the one I unlock." He smiles. Like he's proud of this fact. "It's how we get out!"

"But what's this place?" I ask. Panning a hand to the peaceful valley. It's very picturesque. Almost unreliably beautiful. Like it was painted or something. But it's real, we're here, and I can feel the heat of the bright sun and the coolness of a gentle breeze on my naked body.

Quaid studies the valley down below, then looks around where we're standing on the cliff. He points up. "Look. Is that a village up there?"

I turn and look up in the direction he's pointing. It does, in fact, look like some kind of village. "Where are we?"

"I don't know," he says. "But when you saw us running in the maze, was it that time we were all running together? When we first figured out where we were?"

"No." I shake my head. "It wasn't that time. It was different because we—you and me—we were only half dressed. No shoes. It was like we were interrupted in the middle of sex and had to get the fuck out of Dodge, pronto."

"Do you think that something is happening back in... reality, or whatever? Are Aric and Declan in trouble?"

I shrug. "I didn't get that feeling. In fact, I got the feeling you and I were on a mission. Like, on an assignment. I was supposed to sing the song and you were messing with the glowing symbols on a wall." I let out a huff. "It doesn't make much sense, does it?"

Quaid looks at me and smiles. I think, fully realizing that we're naked. "Feels like paradise to me so, I'm not complaining."

"But it's not real." Again, I pan a hand to the place where we're landed. "This is like a dream."

"Hmm. You're right. It is like a dream. I'm stuck with a naked woman in paradise." He thinks for a moment, looking around a little. Then his gaze meets mine. "Let's think about this logically. The only reason we were having sex is to unlock your power. The one you and I share—for whatever strange reason. And this is what happened. I saw code and you saw..." His eyes light up. "The future!"

"Why would it be the future?"

"Because it hasn't happened yet. You saw... the plan!"

"The plan to escape?" At first, I'm not sure. But the more I think about it, it did feel like a plan. Like I said. A mission. An assignment.

"We need to get back," Quaid says. "We need to get back and tell Aric and Declan because all the puzzle pieces are finally starting to make sense to me."

I let out a long breath. "I'm really glad you're here because it doesn't make any sense to me at all. Most importantly though, how the hell do we get back?"

My question makes him smile as he takes a few steps towards me. One hand snakes around my hip, pulling me right up next to his naked body, while the other goes back up to my throat. He starts walking forward, forcing me to go backwards.

Suddenly, I can feel the roughness of the cliff behind me, and then Quaid reaches down, hooks his hands under my knees, and lifts me up, pressing his stomach right into my open pussy.

Bracing himself against the wall to keep me in place, he reaches down, gives his cock a couple of priming tugs, and slips it right up inside me.

I close my eyes, moaning, and then he's got his hand on my throat again and the stars are back...

The next thing I know, I'm lying down on the bed having the orgasm of my life. My back arching, moans and squeals pouring out of my mouth, and I'm looking up at Quaid as he comes too. His low grunts and growls even more a turn on than his cock.

Then he falls on top of me, spent and happy as he kisses my neck and breasts.

The door to the room flies open and Aric

comes rushing in. "What the hell is going on in here!"

Declan is right behind him, chuckling. "We thought you were killing her!"

"Well," I say. "If I died, then I'd do it all over again. Because we just went to paradise."

20 - ARIC

"What's your problem?" Quaid says.

It takes a moment for me to realize he's talking to me. I point to myself. "My problem? I don't have a problem?"

"Then why are you staring at Star with that look on your face?"

My head turns to towards Star, where I was looking before Quaid interrupted my thoughts, so I guess I can see what he's saying. She's completely naked, looking like a little fuck bunny—which is a compliment in my book—and I'm caught between feeling horny and trying to force my brain to concentrate.

Quaid is naked too. I glance over at him again —his dick is still hard as he rubs a random towel up and down his shaft, cleaning himself off. And he does this like he's the only guy in the room, so it's kinda arrogant.

Of course, I did this as well with the same attitude, but anyway. My point is, I understand why he asked the question. He's wondering if I'm jealous, maybe. Something along those lines, at least. "I was just thinking," I say. "About what you two were saying about the paradise place."

"What about it?" Quaid asks. He's still got a little heat in his tone.

Which I don't care about at all. Whatever discomfort he's feeling over Star is his issue, not mine. I'm trying to focus here. "I'm just trying to understand how we all interact with her in different ways. We all bring out her magic specific reasons, ya know?"

"Or," Declan says, "she brings out something specific in us."

I nod. "Yeah. It could be that too."

"So you're not pissed off?" Quaid asks.

"Pissed off about *what*? You and Star?" I shrug up a shoulder. It is kinda weird that I'm not feeling possessive over her. Especially since I had her first. Technically, she's mine. Like *all* mine. Like I could claim her and that would be the end of it. Well, maybe not. But I'd have every right to put up the fight.

My gaze wanders over to Star and I find her watching me intently. She's got no clothes on and she's not even crossing her arms, trying to cover her breasts. She just stands there, eyes locked with mine, daring me to make a move.

I don't think she'd mind if I tried to keep her for myself. I think she might like the idea that I'd fight for her. And I would, but Declan and Quaid are important and I'm not really an impulsive man, so I say, "We can sort it out later," talking only to her. "Right now, I need them."

"And so do I," she says, tilting her chin up. "I like you all." She looks around, finding Quaid's eyes first, then Declan's, and then finally, her eyes meet mine once again. "I want you." She points to me. "And Quaid. And Declan."

"All right," I say.

"What is happening here?" Declan asks. When I look over at him, I find him making a little motion with his finger between Star and me.

"Nothing," I say. "There's nothing going on between Star and me at all. But there's definitely something going on between the four of us. And that's all I'm thinking about at the moment."

"She made you her safe word," Quaid blurts.

I look at him. "What?"

"Yeah. You. If I got out of control, she said she was gonna call for you."

I glance at Star again with an eyebrow cocked.

She shrugs. "What? You're the son of Ares. Warrior king extraordinaire, or some such shit, right? Who better to save me from an out-of-control moment of heat?"

"*Anyway*," I say, trying to change the subject for like the hundredth time. "As I was saying, there's a real connection between us and—"

"Yeah," Star interrupts. "And it's *sexual*. Between me and all three of you guys. So…"

I blink at her. "OK. Fine. You guys want to have this out? You want to waste time talking about *feelings* instead of plotting our escape? Whatever. Let's do it." I look at Star first. "I'm gonna fuck you. Hard. Regularly. Forever. You're mine. Not only did I claim you first, I fucked you first. Which, under Olympian laws, means you're rightfully mine. So get ready to be ravished three or four times a day. What you do in between those times is up to you."

I look at Declan next. "Enjoy, friend. I think you're a decent demigod and I don't mind sharing with you as long as you respect my claim."

Then I look at Quaid. "If she ever calls out my name when you're fucking her, I will annihilate you. I will rip your cock right off your body and feed it to the hounds of hell. And after that's done, I'm gonna get nasty. There." I throw my arms open wide. "Have I sufficiently displayed my jealous gene? Do you all feel better now that I've acted in character? Are you satisfied? Can we please get on with the escape plan now?"

Declan raises an eyebrow at me. "You're really not jealous?"

I shrug. "Of *you two*?" Which makes him laugh. "Bro, it's not even up to me. It's up to her." I point to Star. "She likes all three of us. She wants to fuck all three of us." I narrow my eyes a little at Declan and Quaid because while Declan hasn't displayed it much, he's got a freak vibe coming off him. And even though I'd have never guessed Quaid was a dom, I can see it now and I'd just like to nip this shit in the bud. "Just don't try your kinks out on me, OK? I am not interested. I don't want reports, or retellings, or play-by-plays. Now can we *please* get on with the business at hand?"

Finally, I think it sinks in because the three of them trade casual looks and shrugs, then turn their attention back to me with expectant eyes.

"Good," I say. "Now listen. Here's how I see it. Star and I together do something to the maze. Probably because I ran this thing thousands of times. I'm connected to it. At the very least, Ares is connected to it and I'm connected to him. I think the glowing walls are saying something."

"The way out," Star adds.

I point at her. "Yes. It's like a cheat. You know, in a game? Because that's all this place is. Just a game. I've been thinking about those glowing symbols on the walls and I think they're some kind of record of my time here."

"How's that work?" Quaid asks.

I shrug. "I dunno. I'm not sure it matters how it works. When Star and I were running, the song would play. Like the wind we created triggered something." Now I point to myself. "I think that was me. The song? It's mine."

"But I've been hearing it since I was a girl," Star says. "Why?"

I shrug. "No clue. Maybe we're... fate, or something? Not sure. But it's definitely my song. You're just attached to it for some reason. But there's more. Because when we came back to the room, it was the past, remember?"

She nods. "How though?"

"Oh!" Declan snaps his fingers. "I think I understand! Star is Pleiades Eight! An actual Star! Which means, she's a timekeeper."

"Hmm," Quaid says. "Now that is interesting."

"Why's that?" I ask.

"Because it makes sense," Quaid says. "Stars keep the time. They are predictable. Their movements can be calculated. Somehow, she controls time."

I look over at Star and find her making one of those 'what-do-know' expressions as she nods. "That does kinda makes sense."

"So she controls time." I point to the floor. "In here, at least. And my song took us backwards."

"I'm not sure how that's helpful," Declan says.

He's kinda right, but I have an idea. "I don't know the way out now, but I did back then. After leaving here, I tried to block it all out. I would not be able to find my way out of here. Not easily. I'm too far removed from it. But if we went back in time—"

"You'd know the route!" Star says.

I make a shrug with my hands. "I think I could do it. The song is a record of all my attempts and those glowing symbols—although I've never seen them before now, I think that's how this place kept track of me. Basically, they're like an exit sign. So all we gotta do is make this place sing and I'll be able to follow the signs."

"So how do we fit in?" Quaid asks.

"You and those glasses of yours are gonna help me. I mean, there's a lot of symbols, right? We need computation power. Otherwise, the Minotaur will get us before we can figure it out."

"What about Paradise?" Star asks. "Why the hell did Quaid and I end up in Paradise?"

I smile. "It's our destination, of course. This maze exists in some kind of... I dunno, magical space. Dimensional space, if you wanna get all scientific and shit. When I finally won, I ended up in a dark space made of nothingness. And then, a moment later, I was back in my bed at home. Only I was five years older."

"Well, we don't want to end up there," Declan

laughs. "That would not go over well with your father."

"No shit," I say.

"But it wasn't real," Quaid says. "Paradise, I mean. It was very dreamlike, don't you agree, Star?"

Star is nodding. "It was. I don't think it was real either."

"It was a possibility," Declan says.

"Exactly," I say, looking straight at him. "Which leads us to you, Declan. The only one of us who hasn't unlocked a power yet by getting Star off. You're our ride, friend. You're gonna get us all out. You're gonna turn that dream into reality."

21 - DECLAN

ou're gonna get us all out.
"Nothing like a little bit of pressure, am I right?"

Star smiles at me. "No pressure. No pressure at all, Declan. All you have to do is what you do best. That's it." She turns to look at Quaid and Aric. "That's the theme here, don't you think? That you're just doing what you do best."

Both of them agree, not looking concerned at all. But they're they beginning and middle of this little escape plan. I'm the actual 'get it done' guy.

Still, I am the messenger of the gods. Well, not exactly. But I'm the son of that guy, which should count for something. Besides, the preliminary step in this little drama that's playing out is sex with the missing Pleiades Eight. In the beginning of this adventure I was hoping to make out and feel her up a little. But she's had sex with both Aric and Quaid—and she's already naked—so as far as I'm concerned, that's my prize whether we get out of this stupid maze or not.

No pressure, Declan, you got this.

Star is smiling at me with a twinkle in her eye that I interpret as a mischievous invitation. I extend my hand, beckoning her to reach for it. She steps forward with her chin high and her breasts all perky and tight. She's sexy with clothes on, pretty as well, but naked, she could give Venus a run for her money. Her curvy hips sway as she approaches me and places her hand in him. "Take me away," she says. "Sweep me off my feet and show me what I'm missing out on, Declan."

I pull her towards me, only marginally aware that Quaid and Aric are watching, but I already know what happens the moment I kiss her from their perspective because I've witnessed it twice now. Star and I are gonna disappear, and end up somewhere cool, and we're gonna fuck. And then, at the moment of climax, we're gonna have a transcendent experience.

My hand slides around her round hip, reaching down to grab her ass as my other arm slides around her back, forcing her breasts to push against my chest.

She giggles, smiling up at me. Even leaning

up on her tiptoes a little. I spy Aric and Quaid leering at us from across the room, and I decide to put on a good show. I take her face in my hands and lean in, kissing her with an open mouth and lots of tongue.

She responds in kind, her eyes closed, moaning into my mouth. And it's like she hasn't been getting fucked all day by other men. Or maybe, her sexual appetite is insatiable. Either way, it's just a big green light to close my eyes and do whatever I want with her.

A few seconds into the kiss, I feel a sort of twirling sensation. Like we're caught in a whirlpool. And when I open my eyes, Aric and Quaid are gone.

Hell, the whole room is gone.

Star's eyes are open now too and she gasps, breaking the kiss and clapping her hands. "Oh, my god! Look at this! I knew you were gonna take me somewhere amazing, Declan. I knew it!"

It *is* amazing. We're still in the maze because the black stone walls look the same as all the corridors we've been in. The glowing symbols are here too, but that's where all the similarities end. It's a circular room with many arched doorways around the perimeter. They don't lead anywhere, they're blocked up with stone, like they're part of the walls. But it's very clear that they *could* lead somewhere.

If you knew how to open them.

"Wow," I say. Walking over to one and placing my hand on the cold, hard stone. "Where do you think they go?"

"To Paradise, of course," Star says.

"And how do we open them?"

She gives me a sideways smile, then bites her lip. "We fuck them open, obviously. I mean. That's how it's been working so far. I kiss one of you guys and then we get all worked up, have some dirty sex, and at the climax, a secret is revealed. Our secret must be the doors, Declan."

I shrug, agreeing. "Makes sense because I'm transport guy." Then I grin and give her a side-eye. "We shouldn't waste any time." I take her hand and pull her close again. Looking right down into her eyes. "How should I lead you into the Land of Bliss, my little hot goddess?"

"What about that?" She points up to the ceiling.

I look up and find a dark, black hole in the shape of a dome. "Huh. I don't know."

"Is it another door?" she asks.

"Only one way to find out." I lean to kiss her again, but she places a hand on my chest. "What's wrong?"

She shoots a quirky smile that immediately sends some dirty vibes my way. "Well," she says, tracing a fingertip a fingertip down the middle of my chest. "Maybe it's my turn to take one of you guys to the Land of Bliss?" And as she's saying this, that finger of hers continues all he way down to the little happy trail that leads into my pants. I look down at her finger, then back up to find her biting her lip. "I really want to unbutton your pants with my teeth." And as she's saying this, she's lowering herself to her knees.

My mouth nearly drops open. I mean, of course I was picturing a whole bunch of hot, sweaty fucking, but I had planned to make all the moves.

However… I am an equal opportunity kind of man and I'm more than willing to let her take control of the situation.

I grab her hair with both hands and watch as she begins to lick my stomach. Her eyes are trained up, locked with mine as she deftly places her teeth over the button of my jeans and then, a moment later, pops it open.

My dick was already getting hard, but it kinda springs to life in a major way at this little trick. "Fuck yeah," I whisper. "I like that."

"Good," she says, "Because there's much more to come." She winks, then grabs my zipper between her teeth and pulls it down so part of my hard, thick cock spills out a little.

My head actually drops backwards and I increase my grip on her hair as her hot breath pulses against my shaft and her hand reaches in to fully liberates the whole length of my dick.

She pumps me a few times. Twirling her

tongue around my tip like it's a sweet little lollipop.

I fist her hair, pulling it a little, but at the same time, pushing her into my stomach. "I want to put my cock in your throat," I say.

And before I'm even done saying that, her mouth closes around me, her tongue pressing up against my tip, and she takes me in. Not all the way, but more than enough to make me draw in a hissing breath.

"You feel so good," I say.

She doesn't respond with words, of course, because my dick is in her mouth. But she bobs her head back and forth like she's nodding. But at the same time, like she's fucking me with her mouth.

That's all the encouragement I need, I get into the motion too. Helping her out so she can concentrate on breathing as I practically suffocate her with my cock.

I don't force her to take me deeper, but with each thrust, she tries. She tries so hard and when I look down, I find that she is still wide-eyed and looking up at me.

"Fuck yeah," I whisper. "Holy shit, you're so hot, Star. Take me as deep as you can. Whatever you have to offer I will accept."

She tries to smile, but her mouth is stuffed and her lips are stretched, so all I see is a tiny upward tilt at the corners of her mouth. Then she opens wider, pressing herself forward without any help from me, and I feel my cock slide down into the top of her throat.

I nearly lose it here. I clench my jaw so hard, trying not to come, I feel my teeth grinding.

I'm nearly back under control when I feel her tongue pressing against my shaft. Undulating and stroking me—and that's it. I can't hold out.

A wave of euphoria rushes through my body and the blood in my dick expands into a tidal wave of pleasure and the next thing I know, my release is spilling out of me and Star is choking on my come.

She sputters, pulling back, and immediately, I kneel down next to her. Kissing her cheeks and grabbing her tits, and easing my hand between her legs, searching for a way to repay her favor.

She lies back on the stone floor so I can hover over her, "Inside me," she says, nearly begging as she opens her legs wider. "Put your cock inside me, Declan. I want it now." She places her hand at the top of her little triangle of hair and slips her middle finger down into the wetness. Stroking herself as, one again, she looks me in the eye.

I smile, nearly grinning from ear to ear, and shake my head as I grab her hand and remove it from her pussy. "No, no, no you dirty little brat. You don't get off that easy. I'm gonna drive you crazy the way you just did me."

She squeals a little, arching her back and pretending to try and squirm away. But I'm hovering over top of her now, so I just lean down a little and take her mind off the games with a kiss. A forceful, hard kiss that comes with some biting. The kind of kiss that's meant to leave her lips raw and sore when it's over.

But that's not the only thing that's gonna be raw and sore.

As I'm doing this, I place two fingers at the entrance to her now dripping-wet pussy and shove them up inside her.

She gasps and arches her back again, only this time it's from the unexpected jolt of pleasure from my finger fucking and not the playful squirming of a dirty game. Soon her hips are moving in the opposite direction of my thrusting and she's getting so worked up, I know my time is short.

I'm not ready for this to be over. I mean, of course I'm gonna fuck her for real after this, but there is much more I can do to her before I actually put my cock in her pussy. So I pull my wet and glistening fingers out and watch her face contort in confusion at the unexpected withdrawal.

"Shhh," I say, prompting her objections. "Don't worry, I'm not done with you just yet." Then I lower my head down between her legs and use my right hand to spread her pussy open. At the same time, my tongue darts out and takes a long lick of her sweet juices. But that's not all—she's getting the full treatment from me. I push two fingers of my left hand back up inside her and then I tickle her little nub until she's gripping my hair with clenched fists and has my head locked between her knees. She's desperately trying to close them to stave off the nearly unbearable wave of pleasure that's now coursing through her blood.

I laugh a little, still licking her pussy as her come begins to flow into my mouth.

She never had a chance.

I let her writhe and get it all out. I let wave after wave of climax hit her until it's nothing more than a small prick of pleasure. Then I lie back on the floor and pull her on top of me. I play with her hair as she gets her breathing under control. Gently sweeping my fingertips over her bare shoulders, which makes her shiver.

We might even fall asleep. I know I doze for sure, but for how long? I have no idea. Time doesn't seem to mean anything. All I know is that, at some point, my dick jumps with anticipation when Star leans her face into my neck. Her breathing is slow now, but I know she's awake.

So I reposition her hips, making her suck in a long breath. "Ready for the grand finale?" I ask.

She hums her affirmative into my ear. "Mmmm. I'm so ready for you to fuck me."

"Put me inside you, then."

Star snickers a little, but lifts her body up enough to reach her hand between my legs. She fists my cock, pumping it a couple of times, and then places it against the wet and ready entrance. Then she slowly lowers herself down onto my dick. She's still so wet from her earlier climax, that my cock slides into her tight pussy like a key fitting in to a lock.

Then she sits up, her hands flat on my chest and her long, dark hair hanging down, tickling my skin. Her hips begin to move slowly at first, but I'm not in the mood for slow. So I grab her tight around the waist and slide her back and forth across my lap as I thrust upward.

Her head falls back, her mouth open, allowing a moan to spill out, and then it's just all too much. For both of us because we come at the same time.

Then we are spinning... floating up into the air. Only we're no longer fucking, we're standing upright.

"Holy shit," Star laughs. "I totally forgot we were here to find our power!"

I laugh too. "Well, I guess it's a good thing that the universe understood the assignment, because we just about failed."

We're still in the same room—it's round with

lots of arches around the perimeter and there's the dome at the top. But now it's looks completely different. The stone walls are still there, inside the arches, but they're kind of transparent now. You can see something on the other side.

"Paradise!" Star says, excitedly pointing to the arch in front of us. "That's Paradise! That's what I saw with Quaid!"

"But, there's still remnants of bricks between us and it, Star. Look. We won't be able to walk through."

"Yeah. How do we—" But she stops, and when I look at her, I find her looking up. "Oh!" She points to the dome above our heads, which is no longer a black hole, but the night sky. "Look!"

"Holy shit," I say. "It's the Seven Sisters. The Pleiades!"

"My sisters!" Star exclaims. She looks at me as we slowly spin in mid-air. "Maybe I draw magic from them and that's how we get past the bricks?"

And just as she says that, the stars above us begin to spin. Wildly. Like we're looking at the Precession of Polaris—which makes a kind of star trail up in the sky in the form of a circle when you speed it up in a time lapse.

Only, we're not looking at Polaris, we're looking at Pleiades.

"Holy shit again!" Star says. And at the same time, there's a grinding noise. We look down and find that the transparent walls inside the arches have all disappeared.

"That's it!" Star says. "My power is to realign the night sky so that the Pleiades are the center of the universe! That's what unlocks the doors to Paradise!"

22 - STAR

My last few words have barely left my mouth and I'm looking right at Declan, when I realize something is different about him. "Hey, what's with your ears?"

"Huh?" He reaches up and touches the little feathers that have sprouted from his ears and sighs. "Oh. That."

"*That?* You have wings on your ears, Declan. I'm gonna need an explanation."

"It's part of the whole messenger thing. Son of Hermes and all that."

"Didn't he have wings on his feet?"

"Yeah, well." He points to himself. "Bastard son, remember? So I get the ears. I hate them, they're stupid. It's got a fairy vibe, don't you think?"

I walk over to him, smiling. I like Declan. I like all three of my new men, but Declan has a sweet spot with me because he feels... I dunno. My age, or something. I'm pretty sure he's probably the same age as Aric and Quaid— around there, at least. But he's got a younger energy. More adventurous than Quaid and far, *far* less serious than Aric.

So I don't like that he hates his ear wings and now I kinda feel responsible for his somber mood after all the fun we just had because I'm the one who brought them up. The wings on his ears are tiny. Like the size of my hand. Obviously, they are not literally meant for flying, but are more symbolic. A physical representation of his powers.

I touch the creamy-white feathers, running my fingertips over them. This makes him shiver, his skin prickling up with tiny bumps. "Sorry," I say. "If you don't like it—"

He grabs my hand when I try to pull it back, looking me in the eye. "No. I do. It feels good. I just don't like the wings. They're embarrassing."

"Why?"

"Because it's just a reminder that I'm the outcast in the family. I have seven half-siblings and while not all of them inherited the messenger gene, the ones that did all have winged feet. It's just me with these dumb ears."

"Huh. You're the eighth?"

He pauses here to reflect., "Uh, yeah. Why?"

"Like me!" I say. "We're both the eighth sibling. We're both outcasts."

"Hmm. I guess that's true."

I place my hands on his hips, hooking my fingers through his belt loops as I smile up at him. "Don't you see, this is what connects us."

His eyebrows go up. "Our status as lesser siblings?"

"Come on, look around, Declan. Tell me one thing about this place, or the experience we're having, that implies we're anything but special? I mean, we're standing inside the Labyrinth looking at a portal that leads to Paradise." I turn, pressing my back up to his chest, and point at the closest archway. "We're gonna go there. And I don't know what it's gonna be like—maybe it's horrible? Maybe it's our own version of the Odyssey? But I don't think too many people make it this far. I mean, Aric ran this maze a thousand times, he said. And he never made it this far." I turn to face him again. "*We* made it this far." I hike a thumb over my shoulder. "And your power is gonna get us there."

"Yeah," he says, smiling now. "That's true. I can't argue with that. Whatever is happening here, it's epic."

"Of course, it is. We're heroes, Declan. Like Odysseus."

He points at me. "And Theseus, your half-brother. He's the one who really killed the Minotaur and beat the maze."

"Did he return home? Or did he find this place and go through to Paradise?"

"Went home. So if he found this place, he didn't go there." He points to the archways.

"Hmm. Makes me wonder why Ares wanted Aric to run this maze so bad."

"Maybe Theseus did find it?" Declan asks. "And maybe Ares heard a rumor or something and he decided to send his bastard son in to map it out?"

"Aric never found this place, though."

"No. He killed this version of the Minotaur and everything ended."

An idea forms in my head. "Maybe killing the monster removes access to this room? Maybe we have to defeat the Minotaur, but not kill it?"

"Or…." Declan counters. "We have to kill it in here." He points to the ground.

I'm nodding. "That makes sense."

Declan stares at the land on the other side of the archways. "It would explain why no one has found that place yet. Because if you think about it, thousands of people have run this maze in real life. I always thought the goal was to kill the monster, and that they all failed until your brother came along and took the Minotaur out. But what if the gods knew something about this

Paradise place and the goal wasn't to kill the Minotaur, just get past it to find this room where the doors are?"

I'm nodding as he talking. "Which is probably the center of the maze."

"What do you think that paradise really is?" Declan asks.

"No clue. But back in the jail, Quaid said some cult was after me, remember?"

Declan nods. "Yeah. Helix, or something."

"Maybe it's not me they want, Declan. Maybe it's this room?"

"Maybe you're the key to the room, Star. Ever think of that? Because it was your brother who killed the Minotaur. Thousands have tried, only he succeeded. Maybe this maze is connected to you by a bloodline?"

"Why wouldn't they just get one of my sisters then?"

He points up to the domed ceiling. "They're up there. In the night sky. And you're not, Star. You're down here. You're the only one they have access to."

I smile, once again reaching up to lightly brush my fingertips across the feathers of his ear wings. "I want to know what's on the other side. Do you?"

He nods. "Yeah. Should we go back now? So we can tell the others and make a plan to get the hell out of this dump and spend he rest of our lives in Paradise?"

I don't even have time to open my mouth to respond before I'm sucked back into reality. Which is a nice place to be, even in comparison to paradise, because I'm on top of Declan and we're still coming.

I'm moaning and writhing, and he's got a death-grip on my hips.

We're back in Aric's room and both he and Quaid are watching as Declan and I finish.

I collapse onto top of Declan's chest and he wraps his arms around me. Neither of us says anything, we just enjoy what's left of the peace we found for as long as we can.

Which is only a handful of seconds. Because Aric says, "Well? What happened?"

Reluctantly, I roll off Declan and we both get to our feet. He hastily tucks away his dick while I scramble around, searching for my clothes.

Quaid is holding my dress. Like he was waiting for my return. He extends his hand, offering it to me.

I smile, sheepishly, because I suddenly remember that I told him Declan might be up for his brand of kink. It's like he's reading my mind because he shoots me a wink, whispering "Was he fun?"

I blush now. But I also nod. "He's very fun, Quaid." Then I wink back.

After I pull my dress on, I turn to Declan, who is already deep into the explanation of what we saw and figured out.

Aric is nodding as Declan explains what we think the maze really is. "That makes sense. And my father must've heard the rumors, like you say, and sent me in to find the way to the doors to Paradise."

"Well," Quaid says, "I guess we've got it all figured out. Now we need a plan to get past the Minotaur without killing it. Which seems harder, if you ask me."

"Not really," Aric says. "Not with all the powers the four of us have collected. The song is a cheat. A map to the whole maze by way of the glowing symbols on the walls."

"But we don't know what the symbols say," Quaid says.

"No, we don't," Aric admits. "But your glasses should be able to decipher them, right? Are they working now?"

"Better than ever, actually." Quaid looks at me. "It seems like the sex really did add to their power. It's so weird."

I shrug. "Well, according to what I learned with Declan, I'm capable of shifting the night sky so I guess upgrading your tech is very small in comparison."

He's nodding at me, but there's a kind of look on his face that gives me the impression that he's not convinced.

Aric must see it too, because he says, "What?" And he's talking to Quaid. "Why do you have that look on your face?"

"It's just..." Quaid starts, but can't seem to find the right words. He starts again, "Don't any of you think it's odd that we're like this... *key* that unlocks a door to another world? How the hell did the four of us end up in the same bar on the same night?"

"Synchronicity!" Declan says, ever the optimist.

"Maybe," Quaid says, but it's very clear he doesn't agree.

"Well, what do you think it is?" Aric asks. "Just say it. I mean, we're about to do something pretty fuckin' dangerous, if you've got concerns, let's hear them."

"I feel like there's a hand guiding us, you guys."

"Who's hand?" I ask.

He looks at me and shrugs. "I don't know."

"Apollo?" Aric asks.

"Or Ares," Quaid shoots back.

"Or Hermes, or Hera, or Theseus, or who the fuck ever," Declan says. "Who cares? We're here and they're not."

"What if it's a trap?" Quaid asks. "What if they sent us in here just like they sent Aric? What if we're the sacrifices?"

None of us say anything. Because this makes too much sense to disregard.

After many long seconds of silence, Aric finally throws up his arms. "Fine. It's a trap. We're worthless fucking demigods and a mortal. That's all we'll ever be… if we stay here. But if we can get to the center and go through to Paradise, we've got a real chance guys."

"And if we die trying?" Quaid asks.

Declan shrugs. "Who cares? If it's true, and the gods all think we're nothing but a bunch of expendables, then fuck them and this place too. I'd rather die trying than settle for being something less."

We all nod in unison.

"Yeah," I say. "I don't even know my parents. They sent me away to live as a human. Fuck this place. I'm done. I want my Paradise."

"Yeah," Aric says, practically growling that word out. "My father can go fuck himself." He looks at Declan. "I'd rather die trying than stay here, safe, but despised." He looks at Quaid now. "What about you?"

Quaid scoffs. "You guys were right about me from the beginning. I'm Mr. Nobody. These glasses?" He points to them. "They're not even mine. Apollo lent them to me. He made me check them out like a fuckin' library book. You have no idea how humiliating it is to beg for jobs from the gods." He looks at me now. "I want to be with you, Star." Then he looks at Aric and Declan. "And I don't mind sharing."

Declan chuckles. Aric kinda grunts.

But all I do is smile.

They are *mine*.

They are all mine.

I point at Declan. "Should I ask about the ear wings?"

"Probably not," Star replies in a whisper. "He's touchy about it."

Declan sighs. "I'm not touchy, I just think it's an insult."

I point to myself. "Do I need this information? Because if not, I'd rather not have to process the story. I've got enough going on without Declan's wing-size insecurities."

Declan scoffs, offended. But Star laughs, getting my sarcasm.

I think I like her. I mean, she's fuckable for sure. But there's a difference between doing things with someone and actually enjoying their company. I can see myself enjoying her company in our future Paradise.

Hell, even Aric gives off a huff at my joke, implying that he sorta gets me. I don't need to like him, but he's not as much of an asshole as I first thought back in the jail. Maybe he's a good guy, maybe he's not. But one thing's for sure, I'd rather have him as a friend than an enemy.

"I'm kidding, Declan. Your wings are cute."

Which makes Star chortle and Aric say, "Enough joking. This is a serious situation. We're about to go into the maze." He lets out a long breath. "You guys need to be in top form. The Minotaur is nothing to take lightly. It's a monster. It's evil, It's—"

But I cut him off here. "It's a program, Aric. This whole place is nothing but… a virtual reality or a simulation." It's probably not either of those things, actually. It's probably something dimensional. Time is definitely a variable and I would not be surprised to find out that it all comes down to zero-point energy. But these three aren't in to technical details like that, so this definition will suffice. "It's not real, that's my point."

"It's real enough that we'll *die*," Aric says.

"Well, that's not technically true," I say. "Yes, we could die. But if your experience here is any indication of what one can expect when they run the maze, we'll come back to life and have to do it again."

Aric is shaking his head no before I'm even done talking. "You don't know that. We can't count on that. One shot, guys." He pauses here to look concerned and serious, meeting each of our gazes one at a time. "We get one shot. If we play like we can't lose, we'll lose for sure." Now he lets out a long sigh, as his eyes lock with Star's. "I like you. I don't wanna lose you. *Please*," now he looks at me. "Please tell me you'll all do your best." He ends this little speech looking at Declan.

Declan nods. "Hey, I'm here for it. I'm all in. I'll get us to Paradise, don't worry." Then he winks at me. "My wings might be little, but they are mighty."

I smile, picturing the scenario that Star put in my head of me controlling the two of them.

He *will* play my game.

The thought of controlling a man has never been a desire of mine. Still isn't. But the thought of controlling Declan and Star together—now that's a fantasy worth fighting for.

"Right," I say. "So here's the plan—we go into the maze, I manipulate the code while Aric guides us towards the center. Once we get there, I do something with the glowing symbols while Star sings the song, and Declan transports us to Paradise."

"OK," Star says. "But... how do you know what to do with the symbols?"

"I don't," I admit. "I can't. Not until I actually interact with the system."

"I don't like this," Aric says. "I feel like we need more preparation."

"More fucking?" I ask. "I mean, hell, I'm up for trying." I wink at Star here, trying to lighten the mood. Because it's very obvious that Aric is worried. And if he's worried, we should all be worried. But worry isn't a helpful emotion. Action is. And that's what my plan is. Action. "But I think it was a onetime thing, guys. I don't know why we're here or who or what is sending us clues on how to beat the maze in the form of sex dreams, but we're not gonna get any more answers until we actually *do* something."

Star is nodding.

Declan is nodding.

Aric is… shaking his head.

Which is frustrating. So I'm just about to put on my Mr. Controlling hat and shake some fucking sense in to him, when Star walks over to Aric and places her hands on his cheeks.

"Look at me," she says. With a long sigh, he does this. "You're not alone this time. You'll never be alone again. We're together now. I'm gonna be with you for the whole run."

Which can't be true. Not if the sex dreams were showing us reality because Star was with me when I was manipulating the lights.

But I don't say that. Instead I say, "And me,

Aric. I'm gonna be with you the whole time as well."

Declan says, "We're all gonna be there for you, Aric. You know the way through the maze. You're our leader. We've all got your back."

After a couple of moments of hesitant consideration, Aric lets out a long exhale. "OK. And I'll be there for you guys too."

"Of course, you will," Star says. And then she leans up on her tip toes—kissing him.

24 - ARIC

As soon as Star's lips touch mine, I feel the shift. And even before I open my eyes, I already know what I'll see.

The maze.

The four of us are no longer in my safe room, but standing in the center of a four-way intersection.

My choices, as far as running this maze, have been taken away. Perhaps whatever is controlling this program knows me better than I know myself. Perhaps it knew that I was going to be the one part of our team who refused the call to move forward.

It wasn't a conscious thought. Yet. But my hesitation and second-guessing was certainly leading there.

"Holy shit!" Declan says, "It's started! We're on!"

"Jokes on me," I mumble. But no one hears me. Quaid is too busy spouting programming details that I simply don't understand and Star is gasping and pointing at the glowing symbols on the walls as he starts fucking with them like they are buttons to be pressed instead of ancient carvings.

Declan is spinning in place, looking up at the ceiling. "We did it," he says. "Look! That's the sky that was in the center of the maze."

I look up and find... well, a sky. A night sky filled with twinkling stars. It runs the entire length of all four hallways. Like the Labyrinth isn't underground, but outside.

"But it's not the center," Declan continues.

"No," I say dryly. "It's not."

"Where are we?" Declan asks. "Do you know?"

I study the symbols on the walls. I don't know what they mean, but some of them are very distinct and make up larger patterns.

This thought makes me scoff because when you think about it, it's like a mirror of the sky above. Each star is but a prick of light. But together, they make constellations.

And isn't that what Star is? One piece of a bigger constellation?

They call the Pleiades the Seven Sisters

because it's easy to see seven of the stars in the cluster without a telescope. But there are more than seven of them. More than eight, actually.

"Yeah," I tell Declan. Pointing at the group of symbols that make up a crude image of a bull. The Taurus? Or the Minotaur? "I know where we are."

"Which way to the center?" Declan asks.

But it's not me who answers, it's Star. "That way." She points, not at one of the possible directions, but at a wall. "I can see through the walls," she says. "And the center of the maze is directly that way."

No one asks her how she can see through walls. She wouldn't be able to tell us anyway. We all just stare at the wall, saying nothing.

This silence goes on for several seconds before I realize they are asking me to find a way. Not to walk through walls, but to lead them through the maze.

All right, Aric. The time for hesitation is over. you're here, there's no way out but through, and you're gonna get these people killed if you do not get your shit together.

"This way," I say, pointing to my left.

But at the same time, Quaid says, "This way," pointing to my right.

"How can that be?" Declan asks. "You guys are pointing in different directions."

"It's this way to the center," I say. And these

words come out with confidence. Mostly because I'm sure of this.

I've been thinking of where the center of the maze might be, since I never found it myself when I was here as a teenager. And there's only one area I didn't explore, so it's a simple exercise in deduction.

The center of the maze is the Minotaur's lair.

And of course, I know where it is because I did everything in my power as a kid to stay the fuck away from it.

"So why are you saying it's this way, Quaid," Declan asks.

"Because the codes are like a map," he says. Which again, makes sense. If the symbols are like constellations. Aren't they just a map as well? "And they're pointing this direction." He gestures to my left.

"We need to split up," Star says, looking at me. "When Quaid and I were in the maze, it was just us two. You and Declan weren't there."

Of course, we weren't. Why would we all be together? That might give us a chance.

"OK," Declan says. "So what's that mean?"

"It means only two of us are getting out of here," I say.

"No," Quaid snaps. "That's not true. There are two ways to get to the center of the maze."

I actually laugh out loud. "Oh, I get it. One team to go this way," I point to my left. "And one team to go that way." I point to my right. "Because the center of the maze is the Minotaur's nest."

"I don't get it," Star says, looking at Quaid for an explanation.

"It's easy," I say. "Declan and I are the bait to keep the monster away from home while you and Quaid open the portal and get out of here."

She makes a face at me. "I'm not sure that's right."

"It's not," Quaid says. "We're not leaving you behind. It's the four of us, Aric. You and Declan *will* be the bait. Star and I *will* open the portal. But we're all going through together."

I'm just about to scoff at that when off in the distance I hear a snort.

My whole body freezes up and suddenly I'm a teenager again. Panicked, terrified, immobilized. Unable to think or see a way out.

Then I can smell it and the fear takes over.

Suddenly, Declan is shaking me. "Wake up, Aric. Snap out of it! We have to go. *Right now!*"

And I'm back in the present, alone in the four-way crossroad of the hallway with Declan.

"Where's Star and Quaid?" I ask, my heart thumping like crazy.

"They ran that way! Come on, it needs to chase us so they can open the portal!"

He grabs me by the arm and starts running, forcing me to race alongside him.

And even though, when I look behind me, I can't see the monster.

I can hear it snorting and growling its threats.

I can smell the stench of its animalistic nature.

And I can feel the pounding of its hooves.

25 - STAR

Something is very wrong with my world.

Quaid and I are running down the hallways, turning this way and that, with him in the lead. But my mind isn't here.

It's with Aric. It's with Declan. It's with Quaid. It's all over the place. And it's almost like I can feel their emotions. Aric's is filled with panic. Declan is afraid, but exuberant. And Quaid's mind is nothing but strategies. Pathways that go here and there, which explains our this-and-that path that we're taking.

Suddenly, Quaid puts his arm out, signaling me to stop. "What's up?" I ask, breathing heavy from the sprint. "Why are we stopping?"

As soon as these words come out of my mouth, I hear yelling! I think it's Declan, and it's more of an excited howl than a terrifying scream, which is a relief.

"Look," Quaid says, pulling my attention back to him. "That's Pegasus!" He's pointing to the wall where there's a cluster of glowing symbols.

"What? I don't understand. You can read the symbols?"

"No, look!" Quaid points out a pattern in the symbols. He's not referencing the actual symbols themselves. "That's Pegasus! Can't you see it? They're constellations! That's what the symbols are! Now we just need to find the Seven Sisters and that's where the portal is!"

Seven. There's not seven, there's eight. Technically more than eight. So why do those first seven get all the glory? Makes me mad.

"Star!" Quaid yells.

"I'm listening!"

"No, you're not. Pay attention. Can you see it? These symbols, they're not letters or words. They're stars." He spins in place, looking up and down the walls, while across the maze somewhere, there's more shouting.

"They're in trouble! We need to help them!" I say.

Quaid grabs my arm, pulling me closer to him. "No. They're grown demigods for fuck's sake, they can take care of themselves. If we go help them, we'll all die. We need to find the Minotaur's lair and open the portal. Then we'll worry about Declan and Aric. Come on, I think I know what's going on here but we need to find the lair so I can be sure."

Then he grabs my hand and takes off running again.

The yelling and hollers of Aric and Declan are closer now, like we're running towards them. Which makes sense because both pathways lead to the same place. He pushes me in front of him, yelling, "Hurry up!"

I run as fast as I can and Quaid slips behind me, like my protector, calling out which way to go as we come upon choices in the maze. "Left! Right! Straight!"

But with each step towards our goal, my mind becomes heavy, or something. Foggy. And then it starts to slip a little because the walls all around me turn into glowing green lines like I saw when we first got here, and slowly they become transparent.

I can see through the walls.

And what I see is Aric and Declan as they run the maze just a few hallways over. The Minotaur is not far behind them and even though Aric is panicking, he's hauling ass. Skidding around corners, zig-zagging his way through the maze in an effort to lose the monster. Declan is right behind him and I get the feeling that he could overtake Aric easily with those wings on his ears, but he doesn't. It's almost like Declan is pulling up the rear to put himself between the Minotaur and Aric.

Suddenly, Aric takes a wrong turn. I don't know how I know, I just do. It's a dead end!

He knows it too. Only a couple steps in and he falters. "Fuck!"

His scream is so loud, Quaid remarks behind me. "Never mind him, Star! keep running!"

I do, I'm running. But my mind is with Aric.

I cannot leave him like that. I don't care if he's not gonna die, just wake up, forced to try again. I'm not leaving him.

I hum the melody in my head for our song. Not the simple da-da-dah tune that's been earworming its way into my brain for almost a decade, but a softer version, like a lullaby.

Aric looks up and around, hearing my song.

"What are you doing?" Quaid asks. "Not yet! Don't sing it yet! We need to find the right symbols or we make a wrong move!"

But I don't listen, I continue to hum. Because this is the only way to save Aric and Declan. The Minotaur is just a few hallways behind the zig-zag path that Aric took, it's seconds away from killing them both.

My song rises in volume, filling the maze with music. And through the walls—just one hallway away from where Quaid and I are running—I see the monster. It slows at first, but then, it stops.

"No!" Quaid yells, reaching behind him to take my hand and pull me forward so I'm in front of him now. "Don't sing it yet! You're calling the Minotaur to us!"

He's right. I am. I look over my shoulder, past Quaid, and find that the monster turning on its hooves, sniffing the air, and then fixes its gaze right on me—like it can see through walls as well. And then, a moment later, it springs forward.

Not down a hallway, but through the walls between us!

I scream, stopping the song, and then get a little burst of satisfaction when the Minotaur slams into the stone wall. Because it's back in place now.

I did that. I took the walls down, drew the Minotaur away from Aric and Declan with the song, and then put them back up when I stopped humming—leaving the Minotaur in a completely different part of the maze!

I did it!

I saved them!

I really did it!

Quaid pushes me, urging me on. "Faster! Go faster!"

When I look behind me and find his face, for the first time ever I see his fear, and force my feet to move.

"Keep going," Quaid yells. "We're almost

there. That's Cassiopeia!" He points to the wall as we rush past.

I'm running as fast as I can, but I'm out of breath. I'm not like, unfit or anything, but I've been through a lot. If I had known I'd be running a maze to save my life, I'd have upped my cardio routine. But as it stands, I'm just not prepared for this level of physical exertion.

And my feet are going slower, and slower, and slower as the moments pass.

"We're almost there!" Quaid yells. He knows I can't run much longer. "Sing it! Sing your song!" And when I look up ahead of us, he's pointing at something. Bright lights glowing on the dark stone walls. "It's Perseus!" he yells as we run past. "Sing it now! Pleiades is coming up quick!"

Aric's words start spilling out of my mouth in loud, shrieky—and very embarrassingly off tune—notes. And when I get to the last line, Quaid's glasses flash a bright light and everything becomes... invisible.

Everything but *us*.

And that's when I realize, we're in the Minotaur's lair. Which is the same room as the portal we've been seeing in our sex dreams. It's circular with a perimeter of arches and on the other side of each arch is a hazy, blurry depiction of what might be our Paradise.

Above our heads is an open-air dome that

afford us a complete three-hundred-and-sixty view of the night sky all lit up with stars.

I look across the darkness and find Aric and Declan staring back at me. Only about twenty feet away, but a moment ago, there were walls between us. Further away is the Minotaur in hot pursuit. It's running in a pattern that clearly indicates that the walls have not disappeared from its point of view.

Declan laughs. "We did it! We fucking did it!"

"Quick!" Quaid yells. "Get in here!"

Declan and Aric haul ass right towards us just as the Minotaur roars around a corner, mere steps behind them, and growls its rage, once it realizes they're gone.

Declan does a little dance as he steps into the lair, but Aric starts hurriedly looking around the room as the shadows flicker across his face, making him look meaner and angrier than I've seen him before.

"What are you doing?" Quaid asks him. But Aric doesn't answer. "Aric, what the hell are you looking for?"

The three of us are watching him. He's frantic, not paying any attention to Quaid's questions. There are piles of things scattered around the lair. Bones, and furs, and clothes, and trinkets. Like the monster has been collecting bits and pieces from all its victims over the years.

"There it is!" Aric yells, his hand deep inside a

pile of bones. He turns to us, holding up a knife made of gold. Then he rushes over and pushes us behind him. "Stand back! This bastard is mine." Then he crouches down into a fighting stance and whispers, "Come on, motherfucker. I'm ready this time."

And that's when the Minotaur comes roaring into the room.

26 - DECLAN

he Minotaur's lair smells of animal, but it's not the sweet smell of horses or even the earthy smell of cattle. It's the stench of decay. Everywhere, there are remnants of past maze runners. Piles and piles of bones, and clothes, and random objects collected over however many centuries this maze has been in existence.

It's not dark, not exactly. But the only light comes from a fire on the far end of the lair. A kind of open-air furnace of some sort. And even though I can't know this for sure, it is just understood that the fire is fueled by the remnants of those that came before us.

No wonder this thing haunted Aric even after he won the game.

He made no effort to hide the fact that it was

the maze and the monster who shaped his present self. And hey, maybe Aric's father was right? Maybe it is the trauma in your life that reveals your character and makes you stronger.

But it's also a pretty shitty thing to do to your own son, bastard or not.

Despite all those years of suffering and distress, Aric looks ready for this final challenge. He holds the gold knife like he knows how to use it and his face, lit up by the glow of dancing flames, reveals a man with a serious intent on doing harm.

I would not want to be his enemy in this moment.

The Minotaur enters the lair, its body covered in creepy, flickering shadows, and hesitates just past the entrance, snorting through its nose, like a dragon.

There is a pause here—almost a slowing down of reality—when the air in the room feels heavy with expectations and charged with potential energy. And in this moment the sky above us—a sky packed with stars—begins to shimmer. Lighting up, very bright, then dimming down into complete darkness. Nothing but black. There's not even a glowing ember from what was the raging fire.

"Oh my god," Star says. "What is going on?"

Quaid makes his glasses shine a light for us and that's when the Minotaur flies through the air in a blind rage, aiming all his savage anger at his old opponent.

Aric dives underneath the monster just before it's about to crash into his chest and takes him out. He rolls out of the dive like a practiced expert and pops up to his feet before the bulky monster can even turn around. Then he attacks, plunging the knife right into the Minotaur's hairy back.

The thing wails like a demon, arching and bucking, trying to dislodge the knife—which Aric is still holding on to, so his body sways back and forth like a banner waving in the air.

Just a moment ago, time was ticking off in slow motion but now, it's on fast forward. So much is happening, I can't even process it. Quaid is yelling at me to do something, but I can't think straight, not with the wails of the raging Minotaur and Aric's battle cries.

Then Quaid's pointing behind me and I realize he's telling me to stop Star! Because she's charging at the Minotaur, screaming her song at the top of her lungs.

The thing pauses, which allows Aric to pull the knife out of its back, and so much blood comes spilling out of the wound, immediately it's forming a puddle beneath the monster's hooves.

"Star!" Quaid yells—and that's when the monster swipes a clawed hand across Aric's chest, sending him careening into Quaid and the last thing I see before we're once again tumbling into complete darkness, are his glasses as they go flying off his face, making everything go dark again.

A piercing scream fills the lair and I'm yelling, "Lights, motherfucker, lights!" because I'm pretty sure that scream belonged to Star!

Then a hand crashes in to my chest, and Quaid says, "Don't just fucking stand here looking dumb and helpless, help me find my glasses!"

Surrounded by complete darkness, and in the middle of a violent maelstrom, I drop to my hands and knees and crawl around, patting the ground with my fingertips, frantically searching for Mr. Nobody's glasses.

Suddenly, the room brightens again, but not because we found Quaid's glasses. He and I are both on our hands and knees, looking up at the night sky above us, twinkling with stars.

Quaid says, "Got 'em," and then he and I stand up, mouths open, looking over at a bloody scene I wouldn't have been able to imagine in my wildest nightmares.

Star is on the ground, pinned to the stone floor because the monstrous Minotaur is on top of her.

Kinda.

It's not wholly on top of her, because it's missing a head.

Said head is being held up by one Aric, bastard demigod son of Ares, in a triumphant gesture of victory. His eye is swollen shut, half his face is black and blue, and there's a gash in his thigh that is spilling so much blood, I would not be surprised if it turned out to be an open artery.

Aric is smiling like he just won a gladiatorial fight. His grin is wide but his eyes are wild with violence. And there would be no way to miss the fact that this is a son of Ares.

"Holy shit," Quaid yells. "Star!" He rushes over, attempting to pull the giant monster off her, but I lock eyes with Aric.

"You OK there, bru?" I ask. Because he doesn't look OK. He looks… crazy. And as if to demonstrate, he growls at me and drops he head onto the stone floor. "You know where you are, right?" I ask, trying to keep my tone light. Because he looks more than crazy, actually, he looks like a man who just… cut the head off the Minotaur. "You're with us, remember?"

Quaid, who has managed to get Star back on her feet—covered in blood though she is—has just turned around. For a moment I'm sure he's going to start spilling insults, but he must see the look in Aric's eyes.

It would be hard to miss, because Aric is

staring right at him and slowly raising that golden knife up like he's about to use it again.

Star steps out in front of Quaid, her arms wide. "Stop," she says. "Stop right now, Aric. The fight is over. You're with us and we're with you. And I told you that you would not have to do this alone ever again so whatever leftover rage you have inside you right now, you had better get it in check, mister! Because Paradise is right over there and Quaid is coming with us!"

This girl, I swear. First she dives into the middle of Aric's fight to help him defeat the monster, and then she's stepping in front of Quaid to save him from Aric's residual rage.

Aric lets out a long exhale and his crazy seems to exit with it. Because his shoulders drop, the hand holding the knife lowers, and he closes his eyes. "Is it over now?"

Aw, fuck. Even I'm touched by his pathetic relief. "Come on," I say, crossing the room towards Aric. "Bring it in for a hug. You deserve it."

To my surprise, he doesn't resist when I take him in my arms and give him a squeeze.

Just as I'm pulling back, he side-eyes me. "Thanks."

But I point to Star. "Thank her. I think she might've saved your life."

Probably not. It's more likely Star's little act

of selfless bravery made things worse, but there's no point in hashing out the details now.

"We won," Quaid says.

And that's when a woman in a long black dress materializes out of the night sky above us and lowers to the ground. She claps her hands in slow, mocking applause. Looking each of us in the eye as she turns in a leisurely circle. "Congratulations. You beat the maze." She pauses here to smile. "Would you like to claim your prize?"

My head cocks to the side as I stare at the woman who just floated down from the starry sky. "I know you," I say.

Even though I don't know her and I didn't plan on saying that, once the words are out, I know them to be true. "I know you," I repeat.

She smiles at me. It's a smile that lands somewhere between creepy and scary. But it's Aric who speaks next. "Nyx," he growls. It's a serious growl and looking over at him, still breathing heavy and covered in blood from the fight, I find him almost unrecognizable. "What the hell are you doing here?"

In the few moments that have passes since the Minotaur's death and the appearance of Nyx, apparently, both Declan and Quaid have found their way over to me. They stand on either side of my shoulders, a little bit in front, as if to protect me.

As if Nyx is a threat.

While the woman does seem familiar, I don't actually know who she is. Obviously, some kind of goddess, but I was never a particularly good history student so what she represents to Aric and our current circumstances, I have no clue.

Nyx is not looking at Aric though, she's got her gaze locked on me. Again, her smile is off-putting, but I can't quite explain why.

I'm just about to start asking questions, when the ground beneath our feet begins to rumble.

"What the hell is that?" Quaid asks, looking down at the ground, then up at the ceiling.

"The Labyrinth," Aric says, still growling as he directs a glaring gaze at the goddess. He steps towards the guys and me, cutting in front of us as if he's taken on the role of ultimate protector, and begins to circle her. "This time it was real, wasn't it?" Aric asks. "The Minotaur is really dead."

"And thus," Nyx says, tipping her head up in a gesture of authority and relaxing her shoulders to fold her hands in front of her long, flowing black gown. "It must crumble. The game has been won."

"By us!" Declan shouts.

Nyx finally directs her attention to someone

other than Aric and me and looks over at him. "That's correct, son of Hermes. You all won. Which is why I'm here. Would you like to claim your prize?"

"What prize?" Quaid asks. After getting to know him in some very stressful situations, I've gotten the impression that Quaid is not a 'riddles' guy. He likes straightforward, logical conversations, so his impatient side is showing. "And what do you have to do with it?"

Slowly her gaze finds his, and at the same time, her arms rise up, her finger stretched out, pointing behind him. Which is behind me, so we all turn and look at the portal.

"Paradise!" I say. "We can go now!"

"Not so fast, little Starling," Nyx says. And again, that creepy smile appears on her face. "You can't pass through as you are."

"Here it comes," Aric sighs, rolling his eyes. "The catch." He makes air quotes with his fingers for those words.

"Indeed, son of Ares, there is a catch when it comes to portal magic. Especially when the objective is..." She trains her gaze right on me. "*Paradise.*"

"All right, let's just get to the point here, can we?" Quaid says, ever the pragmatist. "There's something happening to the maze and I don't like it."

As if on cue, again the ground rumbles deep

beneath our feet. But this time, a crack appears in the stone floor. Not a big one, only about an inch wide, but what the hell? What is happening?

"Fine," Nyx says, shrugging up one shoulder. Obviously untroubled by the shifting earth. "The doors to Paradise are open, but not permeable. Look, see for yourself."

Since the room is circular and there are portal archways around the perimeter, we all find one to study without moving. They are not a clear and open doorway to indicate that we can walk through them, but they are more transparent than they were when we first arrived.

The death of the Minotaur had some effect on their permeability, but didn't open them completely.

"If you want to go to Paradise, you must give up all your godly gifts," Nyx says.

"What's that mean?" Declan asks. But he's not looking at Nyx, he's looking at Quaid. And I find it interesting that the trust between us has developed to such a stage where Quaid is the one we turn to for facts. He's our fountain of logic, I guess.

Quaid is shaking his head. "If you're telling me that I have to give up my glasses to walk through that door to Paradise—"

"What?" Nyx cuts him off. "You don't think

it's a fair trade?" She points to me. "Star isn't worth the price of your rental tech?"

This is a biting insult. By highlighting the fact that his godly gift is borrowed, she basically just called him Mr. Nobody. And Quaid is smart and astute enough to understand this, and for a few moments, he is at a loss for words.

Nyx directs her attention to Aric. "And what about you? Do you feel the silly belt buckle is worth more than a lifetime in Paradise with a woman you could love? A woman who would love you back?" Her eyes dart to meet mine. "A woman who could give you a family? The family you've always craved but were never offered by a god who saw you as something to be cultivated, instead of loved?"

"Who are you?" I blurt. "And why do we care what you think about any of this?"

"I'm the goddess of the night, Pleiades Eight, that's who I am. You live in my womb." She points up at the night sky above her head. It's still twirling, the stars leaving a circular white trail that indicates the passing of time.

I point up as well. "That's *my* power. I saw it. I'm the one who makes the time pass. I'm the one who puts the cosmos on the right track. Because I'm the one who can make the Pleiades the center of the universe."

For a moment, I think I see surprise on her

face. But she quickly hides it before speaking. "You've figured it out then."

"I saw it in the dream. I spin things. And this is how time passes."

"Do you know why the Pleiades aren't the center of the universe? Did your little dream tell you that?" It didn't. But she knew this before she asked the question because she doesn't wait for an answer. "It's because of me. Everything that has happened to you since you were twelve was because of me."

"You?" I say, shocked by her words. "*Why?* Why did you interfere in my life like that?"

"Not just yours," Aric says. "She did the same thing to me."

Nyx shoots him a smarmy look. "Oh, please. Let's be real now. It wasn't me who put you here, Aric. It was your father, Ares."

But Aric isn't looking at her. He's looking at me. "She's my stepmom."

"Whoa," Declan chuckles. "I had no idea."

"No one knows," Aric says, looking back at Nyx now. "She wanted it that way because—"

"Because I was protecting my daughter," Nyx hisses.

"Please tell me that's not me," I say. Feeling ill.

"It's not you," Quaid says. "Her daughter is Eris."

Which makes Declan cackle. "That makes sense, That bitch is nothing but discord and strife. Like literally," he says, his voice playful. "She's the fuckin' goddess of discord and strife."

"Hmmm," I hum. "I see. But what does any of this have to do with me?"

"Excellent question," Aric says. "What is your part in this game?"

But before Nyx can answer, the floor below our feet begins to *roll*. Like it's made of water instead of stone. And I find myself putting my arms out like a surfer, trying to ride it.

"Whatever it is you're doing," Aric yells, "stop it right now! We're not gonna be hurried into a decision because you're playing magic tricks on us."

Again, Nyx does not look concerned about the state of the rolling floor. She lifts her chin as if to imply messing around with the power of earthquakes is beneath her. "This isn't me, you stupid child. This is the death of the Labyrinth. You've killed the Minotaur in his lair, stepson. The game is over and you have won." She pans her hands wide to indicate the room. "Your prize is an open portal."

"Obviously," Quaid hisses. "Tell us something we don't know."

"Like how to get through them," Declan adds.

"I already did," Nyx sneers. "Give me your godly possessions and the doors will open. Each one will allow one soul to pass through. Plenty of doors here for the four of you."

"And you?" I ask. "Are you coming with us?"

She places a hand on her heart. "While I would love to remain your guardian for all of time, little Star, I'm afraid I must take my leave of you at this point. You see, in order for you to pass through, you must give your station of Pleiades Eight back to me. I am the womb of the sky, after all. And as thus, I have to remain behind to keep the stars shining."

Then she looks at Aric. "What you need to give up is that stupid belt buckle. And the knife, of course."

Her gaze finds Quaid. "And, as discussed—your glasses."

"What about me?" Declan asks. "I mean…" He kinda scoffs here. "I don't have any godly possessions."

Nyx laughs. "Of course you do! You're the son Hermes!"

"You mean his ears?" I ask. "What the actual fuck! He's not cutting off his ears and handing them to you!"

As if in protest against my declaration, the ground rumbles so loud, and with such power, that all four of us go tilting sideways. I actually fall over—only Aric's quick grip on my arms prevents me from smashing into the stone floor!

"Well, I'm sure Declan won't mind staying behind," Nyx says. "But the rest of you had better get a move on because the Labyrinth is failing fast."

I look over at Declan, my heart suddenly hurting at the thought of leaving him behind. "No," I whisper. I don't want to say that because it implies that I'm OK with this witch of a goddess taking his power in the form of his cute little winged ears, but I can't help it.

I can't imagine a future, in Paradise or otherwise, where Declan isn't there with us.

He's mine.

Declan lets out a breath, his eyes locked on me. "Before you ditch that knife, Aric, put it to use one more time."

Quaid lets out a breath. "Wow."

Aric, for his part, just stares at Declan for a moment. Waiting for him to meet his gaze. But Declan's eyes remain steadfast on me.

And mine on him. That's how I notice the walls are starting to crumble.

"Do it," Declan says. "Quick. So we can get the fuck out of here."

"Wait!" I scream. "Wait, you guys. We need to talk about this!" A gaping hole appears in the stone floor between Nyx and me, but I ignore it. "I don't know what you're doing here, or why you sent me to live in the mortal realm, but something about this is all wrong! You don't cut off people's body parts to win a game!"

"Don't you?" Quaid asks. And when I look

over at him, he's pointing across the room at the Minotaur's head.

"But—" I don't know what to say to that. I just know that everything about this felt right until the Goddess of the Night appeared.

And now it feels wrong.

The archway behind Nyx, suddenly crumbles. Like actually disintegrates into tiny grains of sand.

We all start looking around at the other doors because we need four of them to get us all through and there were only eight to begin with.

Seven now.

And just as I think that, another one turns into sand.

"You'll get them back, you know," Nyx says. Her words more hurried now since the place is literally starting to crumble.

"Get what back?" Aric answers.

"Powers. Different, because they'll come from the old gods instead of the new ones. But everyone who goes through becomes immortal in that realm too."

Another door disintegrates and now we're down to six.

"Ok, everyone," Declan shouts. "Fuck this, we're out of here. Aric, cut off my fuckin ears! I don't care if I look like a mongrel on the other side, at least I'll be there!"

Aric walks over to Declan, already stripping

off his belt and throwing it at Nyx's feet. He holds the knife up to Declan's head and…

Well, Quaid grabs me, pulling me into a hug and turning my head away so I don't have to watch.

Declan screams, and I force Quaid to let me look.

He's covered in blood, but he's wingless and an archway opens for him. "Come on!" he yells. "Let's go!"

Aric throws his knife at Nyx and the moment it clangs against the stone, another archway opens so he can pass through.

"Glasses, Quaid!" Aric yells. "Now!"

But before he can take them off, another archway turns to sand. Five. We're down to five.

Quaid throws his glasses at Nyx, and a third door opens.

Now it's my turn. But I don't know how to give up the essence of myself. So I don't do anything, and it's during this hesitation that the fourth door disintegrates.

And now there are just enough.

Nyx walks over to me, placing a hand on my cheek, and gazes down into my eyes. "You will shine brighter in their lives than you ever could in the heavens. Give it up, little Star. Give me, the mother of the twinkling night, your station in the sky."

Then she opens her mouth and I feel

something come loose inside me. The next thing I know, my mouth is opening too. And I watch as a glittering bit of light comes out and hovers in the air between the goddess and me.

I reach for it, wanting to hold it in my hand. To feel the gift the gods gave me. Because I never knew it was there.

But Nyx leans in and gobbles it up!

She ate my light!

Then, the whole room begins to shake and she flies upward, into the twirling night sky, and the last thing I see of this world before Quaid pushes me through my open archway to Paradise, is an eighth sister lighting up inside the Pleiades cluster.

Everything goes dark.

My world becomes emptiness.

And I knew it. I knew it! I knew there was something fishy about that bitchy goddess! She's probably evil! She did rip me out of Olympus, took my memories of my true self, and left me for dead in the mortal—

But before I can finish my internal rant, the brightest of light flashes, blinding me so I have to put my hands over my eyes. I start to spin. Slowly, at first. But as I begin to rise up into the air, the spinning becomes faster, and faster, until I am a vortex of starlight.

I open my eyes, looking up at a night sky above me.

Twinkling stars make patterns in the chaos.

Three moons shine brightly, but each are in a different stage of luminosity. One is big and dull, but also full. The second is bright and small, and in the shape of a crescent. The third is only half lit, but you can see the rocky terrain, even with the naked eye.

I am transfixed by the beauty of it all, not paying any attention to what's below me until Quaid yells, "Holy shit, Star! Get your ass down here before you fall out of the fucking sky!"

I look down and there they are!

All three of my guys!

Declan laughing like a lunatic, dancing around like a fool, because he has grown a massive set of fluffy gold wings!

Aric is looking down at himself in awe, because he's now wearing the shiniest set of golden armor the heavens have ever seen.

And Quaid, always so bossy and demanding, is looking up at me with glowing eyes! Gold, like Declan's wings and Aric's armor.

Which makes me sigh.

Because we're really a team now.

We're really together. We even match.

I start to descend, making a lazy, twirling vortex until my feet are on the ground. But when I look at my guys, they are not looking at me, but at something above my head.

"What's wrong, is my hair messed up? Did I

go gray, or something? I wouldn't put it past that stupid Nyx." And then I'm ranting again, just like I was in the darkness.

But Aric points to my head, while Quaid puts a hand over my mouth, and Declan says, "Look up, Star. You're... *twinkling.*"

Slowly, my eyes roll up and I gasp. I reach up with my fingertips and find that there is a crown on my head. I pull it off so I can see it, and hold it font of me.

Stunned, I just stare at the twinkling lights. Like teeny, tiny fireflies, except they're... *stars.*

I look at Aric in his golden armor—a sure sign of godly strength if ever there was one.

Then Declan, and his golden wings—certain that they will carry him to wherever he needs to go with exceptional speed.

Then Quaid, with his glowing gold eyes. He smiles at me. "Mr. Nobody?" Then he laughs. "Not anymore. Fuck the glasses because I don't need them. I've got these now." And he points to his eyes.

I look back down at my crown. "What's it mean?" Then look back up at the guys.

"What's it *mean?*" Declan laughs. His gold wings rising up above his shoulders as a way to express his amusement.

"It means you're our queen, Star," Quaid says. His eyes glowing like the crown in my hands.

And when I look at Aric, he bends over into a shallow bow, offering me his hand.

I take it, and the other guys crowd in around me we take our first steps into our new life in Paradise.

I am a queen with three kings.

Mine.

EPILOGUE - DECLAN

*I*t's still dark when Star crawls into bed next to me. I am not fully awake, but I reach over, pulling her into my chest out of instinct and wrapping her up in my beautiful gold wings. It's my day and I like to take advantage of every moment.

She snuggles her face into my neck, kissing the sensitive skin just below my ear. This sends a chill of pleasure through my body and I reluctantly open one eye to peek at her.

"Good morning," she whispers, right into my ear. Then she bites my earlobe.

I smile with satisfaction. Still astonished that we're here, in Paradise. Living together, and sleeping together, and pretty much doing everything together.

"Do you want to sleep," she asks. Her question nothing but a tease.

I respond by flipping her over and leaning down into her face. We lock eyes just before we kiss and in this small moment, I just count my blessings. So lucky that she is by my side.

When our lips touch, her hands begin to wander. Her fingertips tracing down my stomach until they get to the little happy trail that leads to her reward.

I'm naked, of course. Ready for her, and this moment. Because it's my day. The day where all Star thinks about is pleasing me. Her hand grips around my shaft, giving it a tight squeeze.

She pushes me over, on to my back. Her hand pumping up and down my cock as she straddles my legs. I open my eyes as the sun rises, shining just a tiny bit of light though the large window of my bedroom. I want to see her in the golden hour, all lit up and glowing.

Her glorious, naked body doesn't disappoint. Her tits are full and bouncing a little as she jerks me off, staring right into my eyes. I reach for them, cupping them in my hands and giving them each a little squeeze. But as she picks up the pace of her hand job, I let my fingertips slide down to her nipples and give them a pinch.

Star winces, but she likes it. I've noticed things about her sexual appetite since we got here. I don't think much about the time she spends with Quaid, but I'm not gonna lie—I absolutely enjoy the fruits of his labor. Because Star brings all the dirty desires that time with Quaid awakens right into our bed.

The nipple pinching is just a tiny bit of all the new kink she's into now.

I grab her hair and pull her down to me. Making her pause the hand job so she can brace herself on the bed.

We kiss for a little bit. Her belly lowering down to touch mine. Her hips wiggling to keep my cock occupied. She always starts our time together with me. All her attention on me and my pleasure.

In fact, they all do. This is how it is now. When it's my day, it's *my* day.

Aric will make us breakfast.

If I'm doing something, Quaid will offer to lend a hand.

It was weird, at first. Because it was so natural. Which sounds like a contradiction, but I just wasn't used to being the center of attention and when it's my day with Star, that's what I am.

Everything revolves around me and all three of my partners make sure I feel their commitment in some way. Even if it's just a small way.

Star is kissing me again now. Her hips positioning over mine.

I know I share her, but when we're together, I feel like the center of her world.

My dick slides into her pussy, all wet and tight for me, as the room darkens, and the ceiling becomes the night sky, and we make love under the starlight.

She is the light in the night for me.

EPILOGUE - QUAID

aiting for them to appear in the doorway of my room is agony, but I force myself to be patient. Which is not typically one of my strong suits, but the reward I'm going to get is worth the effort.

A door opens somewhere else in the house. I'm not sure where they're at right now—his room or hers—all I know is that they're coming to me.

Both of them. Star and Declan.

Because it's my day.

When Star and I approached Declan to see if he would like to get on our little game, I *did* expect him to agree. Eventually. But I didn't expect him to embrace it.

But he has.

I almost can't believe it. He absolutely gets off on *me* telling *him* how to fuck Star.

She gets off, I get off, we all get off. There's so much getting off, I'm almost expecting Aric to get jealous of all the getting off we're getting and ask to join in.

But he won't. And that's OK. This little fantasy of mine with Declan and Star has just started and I won't be bored with it any time soon.

There's whispering down the hallway now. Declan giving Star some last-minute instructions, I bet. I gave him a very specific scenario this week. A scenario that involves a leash, a collar, and a master, slave, pet relationship.

I grin just picturing it in my mind and I'm so eager to see how they pull it off, my cock is already hard.

I'm holding my breath when Star appears in the doorway to my room. She's on her hands and knees, naked. Her head is lifted, her eyes locked on mine, and her back is nice and arched so her tits are pushed forward.

She wearing a collar. Not the one I put on her back in the Labyrinth—that fell off when we passed through the portal to Paradise—but a new one that Aric made. It was a nice gift. He presented it to me last week when it was my day. Just a way for him to show he cared.

That's why it's part of my fantasy this week. He doesn't join in, but he's still here, isn't he?

It means something to me.

Once I told him my fantasy with the collar and what I was going to make Declan do, he made me a leash to match. So that collar that Star is wearing it connected to Declan by this very leash.

She crawls through the door and Declan comes up behind her. He's naked too. His dick so hard, and thick, and ready for what I will make him do to Star, my own cocks jumps inside my tight jeans.

I beckon Declan with a finger. "Come here, slave. Show me how well you've trained my pet."

That's our scenario. He's my slave and he trains my pets. Today he is presenting this pet to me in order to showcase her obedience.

It could go one of two ways—Star gives in and does everything she's told. Which is going to be quite the experience for her and us. So if she is compliant, we're all gonna have fun.

But she could choose to disobey Declan. In which case, I get to punish them both. Which would also be fun for all involved because when it comes down to it, I'm really just a pleasure man. I just like to control how it happens. So there is no possible way any of us leave this room less than satisfied.

Declan snaps the leash, making it crack

against Star's bare back. But he's got a little whip too, and he smacks her bare ass just for the hell of it.

Star crawls forward on her hands and knees, her eyes still locked with mine. She winks at me, breaking character, then licks her lips, absolutely disobeying because she knows this is against the rules.

So… defiant Star it is.

I force myself to hide my grin, and my pleasure at her choice—because it's always her choice how these scenarios play out—and wait as she finally finishes crossing the room and places her chin between my legs.

I hold absolutely still as Star's mouth comes into contact with my cock. Her look up at me when she sticks her tongue out and begins to lick it through my jeans.

Declan cracks the whip across her bottom, making her squeal. And when I look up at him, he's pulling one of those half-smiling, half-wincing expressions. Like he's not sure if he crossed a line or not.

Star moans and begins wriggling her ass, taunting him.

Declan, in response, grits his teeth and mouths the word, "Fuck!" at me, because he's so turned on right now, he might explode.

This is the first time we've done the whole

master, slave, pet scenario—which must be his thing because I've never seen him so worked up.

But he pulls himself together, barks a few orders at Star—lick me, suck my dick through my jeans, crawl up my chest and kiss me—and every now and then cracks her ass with that whip, even though she's mostly complying.

We're not gonna make it much further, we're all too worked up and horny. So I simply give in and point to Declan. "Fuck her."

He pumps a fist, mouths the word, "Yes!" as he looks skyward, and then kneels behind Star's ass, spreads her cheeks, and thrusts his cock into her pussy.

She jolts forward, into my chest to the rhythm of his fucking and I just watch, daring either of them to come before I tell them they can.

They hold out for a couple of minutes, but I know it's too much. We're all too excited to care about the authenticity of the scenario—we'll worry about that next time.

But for now, I open my pants, pull out my cock, and then grab Star by the hair and push her mouth down over my tip.

Then I let Declan fuck me with Star's mouth as he thrusts his cock in and out of her pussy, and I wonder which god I need to pledge my undying loyalty to for sending me to Paradise.

EPILOGUE - ARIC

*M*y time with Star begins the same way it does with the other bros. She comes into my bed in the middle of the night—naked. And she is always eager to please me in whatever way I desire. It's like my pleasure is her pleasure.

It's nice. Almost normal.

But it's what we do outside the bedroom that turns me on the most.

We never wear clothes on our day because I don't have work. We even walk around the house naked. Unashamed when Quaid or Declan notice.

They like it. I mean… I like it when she's with them. Because fuck yeah, I listen at the door when she's screaming Declan's name. And hell yes I take a peek into Quaid's room when he's making Declan and Star bow to his will and whims.

I like that they enjoy the spectacle that Star and I put on. I mean, what's the fun of walking around naked—all hot and bothered, and wet, and hard—if there's no one around to see?

I might be a bit of an exhibitionist.

But I'm in the right place for that because this world we landed in? This Paradise? Turns out, it's Tartarus. The actual prison of the Titans. Which isn't a prison because, obviously, it's Paradise.

Anyway, the point is... the Titans are all exhibitionists. I've seen dozens of Titan couples sneaking into the bushes for a fuck or ducking into a bathroom stall for a quick blowjob. At first, I didn't know what to think about this. But then I realized that they always made sure that someone was watching them before they do this stealing away.

There'd be some kissing. Then a little petting. His hand would find her leg under a table and pull it over to his dick, helping her jerk him off a little. Or maybe the woman would be wearing a dress and would open her legs under a table, and slip his hand between them.

Figuring out that this was a thing here—that sex to a Titan was a presentation best observed by others—awakened something inside of me. A desire to fit in... maybe?

I mean, what's the point of being an exhibitionist if you don't have a voyeur to appreciate your performance?

So far, no one's done anything right out in public, but if they did, I certainly wouldn't object. It's kind of my duty to participate as their voyeur.

When Star and I hone our performance and take it public, I certainly expect people to be watching.

When we got to Paradise, the residents here came to greet us. A crowd of about fifty came down the hill from the village and made introductions.

Of course, they knew the portal was there. They had all come through it to get here. But it had been a very, very long time since anyone new appeared.

We were welcomed into the village. They set us up with a house big enough to accommodate our arrangement, and then, over the course of a couple of weeks, we integrated. There's a war college here and, as the son of Ares, I was invited to speak to the students about Olympus, and the Labyrinth, and how I defeated the Minotaur.

I'm like… a professor.

Which is weird, but not in a bad way.

Especially since college campuses are a hot bed of exhibitionism. And the students are very serious about making it hard for the voyeurs to find them. It's like a challenge, I think.

It's fun. I like the atmosphere.

Though, as a respected member of the faculty, I don't partake in the game.

Shortly after I settled in to collegiate life, Quaid had me make an introduction to my colleagues in the Tech College. He works there, trying to replicate the glasses Apollo made for him even though he doesn't need them anymore. His organic eyes do everything they did, and more.

Declan, not wanting to be left out, forged his own path ahead by approaching the portal masters. He is the son of Hermes, after all. I'm not sure what he's working on over there, but he seems happy with it.

And little Star?

She's the happiest of us all.

EPILOGUE - STAR

$\mathcal{I}$n the weeks and months following our trip into paradise, the men and I have settled in to a mutually valuable multi-partner relationship. Being with them in this way is like a dream. It really is my own personal Paradise.

At first, when Nyx showed up, I was convinced that it was all a trick. That she just wanted our godly gifts for herself and somehow, some way, we'd all end up the losers.

But I was wrong. Not just a little wrong, either. But next level wrong. Because while we did all have to give up our gifts—and for Declan, this meant giving up a body part—we all got a gift back.

Just like Nyx said we would.

That's really why we settled in to Paradise so quickly.

It was Aric's golden armor that drew the attention of the War College. I still can't believe that our Aric is a professor. But it suits him. And while he thinks that Declan, Quaid, and I don't know that he secretly spies on us when we're all together, we do. Maybe one day he'll join us, but probably not. And that's OK too. I will take Aric any way he lets me. He's still the one who makes me feel the safest. Like he would be there, standing between me and any enemy, and no matter what, I would know that I would be OK when the battle was over.

And it was Quaid's golden eyes that got him the meeting with the tech college after Aric made an introduction. Although, I don't share any powers with Quaid anymore, he's told me that his new eyes give him even more information than his Apollo sunglasses. He tells me that the stars above him are a code, just like the stars in the Labyrinth. And this code is the meaning of life itself. And these new eyes of his will be able to solve the mystery of everything one day. With Quaid by my side, I always feel in control. Because he's always in control. It's very stabilizing.

Declan's new wings give a whole new meaning to the word 'loved'. They are magnificent, and gold, and fluffy, and massive, and he uses them to hug me tight when we're spooning in bed. When he's not in bed with me, those wings take him places. All over Paradise, even places the Titans, who have been here for thousands of years, don't know about. Declan shows his devotion to me by sheltering me in his wings and telling me stories about his travels. When we're together, I feel as if we're a part of history now. A god and his goddess in the making. And one day they will tell tales about us and we will be written in the stars forever.

And even though I gave myself to Nyx when I left the mortal realm, it was a fair trade. Because it was an impossible trade. Pleiades Eight is not a god's gift. It's just... me.

Yes, I gave her my inner light, the star inside me, so to speak—but that light is nothing without the woman it belongs to. It's just a spark. A potential for something not yet realized.

I know this for sure because the starry crown on my head floats above me like a brand-new night sky filled with all new constellations—a universe that paints a picture of all of us.

We are the future.

Because we have been written in the stars.

A Warrior.

A Seeker

A Traveler.

A Queen.

END OF BOOK SHIT

Welcome to the End of Book Shit. This is the part of the book where I leave comments about what you just read. I've been doing this since my very first romance book published in 2013. Most of my books have them, so… the tradition continues.

THIS BOOK here is a product of my Patreon. I started a Patreon a little over a year ago (This is late October 2025). And I had a lot of books that had been written, but not yet released, because I was trying to sell my ranch. Which was a fucking process that took about a year and a half from start to finish. It dominated my life from January 2024 until the house sold on July 2025. Anyone who's been through the process understands that selling a house is a big deal—but selling a ranch is a whole other level of Hell. :)

ANYWAY—THERE is not enough space in this EOBS to fully tell the tale of selling my ranch. Another story for another time.

The point is, I was busy. I didn't have anything to release to my Patreon last fall—I actually think it was last November, so pretty much one year ago. So I did a "Write a Book with Me" month and I let all my Patreon members choose what kind of story they wanted.

I WAS super surprised when they decided on Why Choose. I have kind of written some 'Why Choose' in the past – The Turning Series is definitely Why-Choose-ish. Taking Turns, etc. But I honestly don't pay attention to trends, or tropes, or pretty much anyone or anything in the fucking world of romance books, so I didn't do that on purpose. lol It was just my story and I wrote it.

AND, of course, I was one of the original Indie authors writing dark menage romance back in the early to mid-teens. So I did a lot of those. But again, none of that was on purpose. Never did I sit down and say... OK, I'm gonna write a menage or I'm gonna write a Reverse Harem. That's really not how writing works for me. A story gets sent to my brain and then I sit down and write it. That's pretty much the process.

So I HAD NEVER ATTEMPTED to write a true Why Choose. I actually had to consult Chat GPT about this genre, lol. There was a whole convo with the AI about what the expectations are etc. It explained it pretty thoroughly, so that was nice. It helped because again, I don't write anything 'on trope'. And other than HEA and no cheating, I do not follow any content rules when I write a story.

I DO WHATEVER I WANT. If ever there was a motto about my life, this is. I do whatever I want. Period.

THERE IS no amount of cancel culture or bullying that could make me change something in a story. I do not bend the knee for anyone, especially random people I don't know. And when it comes to my writing, the stories are mine. The art is mine. The product is mine. And that has nothing to do with readers.

BUT... this group here, these Patrons, they're not just readers. They're friends. Most of them I've known for over a decade. Many of them I've met in person. A few dozen of them, I've met in person many times, had dinner with, had them up to my hotel room during signings... etc.

So I DID care about meeting their expectations. Especially when it was "Write a Book with Me" month. Because this was their story.

THEY PICKED THE GENRE, the heat level, the characters names etc. We did do some cover choosing, but there was so much time from the first round of covers to this point right now when I actually needed a cover, that I ended up redoing it slightly. The concept remained the same though.

THEY DID READ along with me as I wrote—something I do not ever do. I'm not one of those writers who will post a chapter as I write. I know many writers do that for their Patrons, but

I don't ever post anything until the story's been through many rounds of editing. Not because of grammar, or anything like that—Just FYI—grammar is not my job—that's the editor's problem.

MY JOB IS to write a good story.

BUT I WRITE books for a very specific kind of reader and I do it in a very specific kind of way. Many things change in the story from first draft chapter to final product. I'm def not one of those people who make several complete drafts of a story—what I write the first time, for the most part, is what actually gets printed.

BUT THE CONTINUITY of the story always needs to be ironed out once the first draft is over because, in case you haven't noticed, my romances are pretty complicated.

SO RELEASING CHAPTERS as I wrote was new to me. I didn't like, I will say that. And unless we do another "Write a Book with Me" month, I won't do it again. It's not pressure that I mind. I am pretty much un-fucking-flappable when it comes to stress. It's just, what you read in the first draft isn't the story. It's just the idea.

IT TAKES me many chapters in to a book to actually understand the story that was sent to my brain for production. Sometimes, in fact, I would say most of the time, I do not really understand what I wrote until it's done. I've read many a review where readers have stated something factual about my story that I didn't even know was in there.

THE STORY IS THE STORY. I really don't have any control over that. I try my best to insert themes and shit—and I do. But what I 'think' is the theme and what the theme actually is at the end, are very often two very different things.

I DIDN'T GO in to this story with any theme because it wasn't my story. It wasn't sent to me, it was crowd-sourced. So whatever theme is in here is news to me.

AND IF I'M being perfectly honest, The Star We Share is just a fun romp through a fantasy sex maze.

. . .

THAT'S all it was ever meant to be and I hope you enjoyed it.

I ACTUALLY DID VERY MUCH ENJOY this story. I like the men and Star and I left the ending open for more books if I ever wanted to continue this world. Of course, there's a maze, of course there's portal magic, of course there are gods and goddesses…

ALL THESE THINGS ARE 'ON TROPE' for me as an author. And while I was writing this, I was also writing/finishing Sparktopia. Which had a lot of the same elements, but on a much bigger, grander scale. And I had just finished the Monsters of St. Mark's series, which was where the whole gods and goddess thing really took root for me.

I WAS, in fact, OBSESSED (at the time) with another story in my head about a maze. It's a massive story that I will write once I finish up the Game of Gods series (Sparktopia, Godslayer Outlands is coming in 2026-2027, unsure about that release date, actually because producing those audiobooks is an epic process).

So this was kind of a practice maze story for me. Nothing AT ALL like the one that's coming, but it was good think about the limitations of a maze story.

I haven't written super spicy novellas since the 2014 Social Media series. I view short, spicy novellas as 'Midnight Snacks' and I am typically more of a 'Formal Dinner Party' kind of author.

But there is something satisfying about writing short and spicy so I will actually be releasing a lot more 'Midnight Snacks' in 2026. One a week, actually. I've got a whole series in my head about men falling from the sky… :)

I'm not an anti-snacker. I like a good Midnight Snack. And I really like short standalones that combine into a series. So, all in all, this little experiment was a complete success from my viewpoint. Whether people like the story or not, I don't really care. It was fun to do, my Patrons got to participate, and I made a full-cast audiobook (and got to try out four new-to-me narrators!) so that's super cool.

TODAY, once I'm done with this EOBS and I've uploaded the pre-orders for ebook and audio, I'm going to send my Patrons the final product and the audiobook tiers of my Patreon will all get to hear the story for the first time.

BY THE WAY—AUDIOBOOK listeners! If you like these narrators, please let me know in your review and I will use them again!

AND THAT'S IT, I guess. The Star We Share is here, my life has settled into a new space, in a new place, and I'm really happy with where I am right now.

I AM super de-dooper excited about getting back to work after many, many, many months off!

(I WAS RV-ing around the country for a few months after the ranch sold, so truly nomadic!)
    It's good to be home.
    I'm thrilled to be back.

Thank you for reading, thank you for reviewing, and I'll see you in the next book.…

(WHICH IS PROBABLY gonna be a Midnight Snack, but oh, my loyal readers, that's just where 2026 starts. You can expect between 7-10 Formal Dinner Parties from me in the coming year. Five of them are already written and in audiobook production.)

Julie
JA Huss
October 29, 2025

One More Thing!

If you like Giveaways I run a **MASSIVE 12 DAYS OF GIVEAWAYS** every December (Dec 1-12) on my website www.jahuss.com and I would LOVE if you came by to enter! Each day there is a new prize and each prize is worth between $150-$250. I will be giving away special edition paperbacks of this book! Come by and say HI!